About the Author

I authored sixteen textbooks and an editor asked if I had a novel in me. This unearthed a revelation… when a scientist restricted to science-fact is released to flirt into science-fiction, interesting things start to happen. My character needed a tech, I developed a solution that modeled too well, leading to a start-up, fifty patents, and acquisition by a Fortune 500. I would live out many parts of 'The Mandate' as if a future-echo came to call, and if my mind were read it would be impossible to distinguish what is my principal character James and what is Nigel.

The James Moore series by Nigel Cook
The Guardian
The Collective
The Mandate

The Mandate

Nigel Cook

The Mandate

Olympia Publishers
London

www.olympiapublishers.com
OLYMPIA PAPERBACK EDITION

A CIP catalogue record for this title is
available from the British Library.

ISBN: 978-1-80439-567-7

This is a work of fiction.
Names, characters, places and incidents originate from the writer's
imagination. Any resemblance to actual persons, living or dead, is
purely coincidental.

First Published in 2023

Olympia Publishers
Tallis House
2 Tallis Street
London
EC4Y 0AB

Printed in Great Britain

Dedication

To my wife, Alonna.

Acknowledgments

Thank you, Dawn, for the hours. And thank you Irene, for the guidance.

Chapter 1

What forces must have been at play to shape the Adirondack Mountains into a dome rather than an elongated range, five million years ago? Ancient rocks, one thousand million years old, were used to create this circle that was one hundred and sixty miles wide and one mile high, which accounts for why the Adirondacks' natural enceinte is described as *new mountains from old rocks*. Cumulonimbus clouds hovered over the mountains as if attached, and unlike their cumulus cousin that foretold fair weather, upper-level winds sheared the tops of these clouds to shape them like an anvil, forecasting that the mountains' blacksmith would soon be at work hammering the area with a maelstrom of thunder, lightning, hail and high winds.

Nathan, layering a jacket over a simple t-shirt and jeans pointed out the window of the Learjet as it banked, to a twenty-acre parcel below.

"On the surface it's a rather basic Lake Saranac Mountain getaway home, nothing special — about two-thousand square feet, I believe."

His fellow passenger, Erik, who was casual today in dark pants, a button-down collar shirt and blazer, looked down at the lodge with its wraparound porch, flanked by a long airplane runway strip leading to a hangar.

"But below the hardwood floors of this home is an eight thousand square foot Cold War missile silo built in 1961. Even if it received a direct nuclear attack from a Soviet first strike, or if it was attacked by ground forces, the personnel were protected and therefore able to launch their Atlas intercontinental ballistic missile. They called this deterrent MAD, mutual assured destruction, but it worked."

Erik took another look. "How interesting. You would never know from up here."

"Engee is on site full time now, with a large security detail guarding them. They are locked away in what his girlfriend called an oubliette — I had to look it up. It means a secret dungeon that only has access through a trapdoor in the ceiling. She's French you know."

"I didn't know that."

"He has his lab, and they've hired a lot of new personnel, closely vetted by us of course. It couldn't be better — he's trapped in an underground industrial complex with unrivaled security."

"Do not underestimate him, Nathan. We locked him away once before, also in an oubliette by coincidence, and he worked his way out. He is irritatingly inventive, and this girlfriend sounds just as annoying."

"I understand, but the aunts make this work. Even if he could get out, he has no idea where we are holding them, and this forces him to comply — it's just like MAD!"

"This is why I'm nervous. Just when you think you have him, that's when he'll surprise you."

"Not this time!"

Erik shrugged, "Stay vigilant."

They touched down, disembarked, and entered the house. Guards led them down a one hundred and twenty-five-foot stairwell to a floor and walls made of three-inch thick concrete reinforced with embedded steel mesh. The original equipment was still there — control panels and monochrome monitors, clocks displaying time zones for three continents, and the hazard symbol for radiation everywhere. Nathan pointed to the equipment as they passed. "Funny to think my smartwatch has more computing power than this whole room's equipment combined."

Down to another level with suites, a gym, swimming pool, Jacuzzi, sauna, and a dining area, all fully staffed. As they continued beyond these two levels, they passed through another security checkpoint and then entered a set of two-thousand-pound blast doors to a seventy-foot tunnel giving access to the actual missile silo — a nine-level cylindrical structure measuring fifty-feet in diameter and one hundred and eighty-five-feet below the surface.

Yet another security checkpoint, and out emerged Engee who showed them into a conference room. She was wearing a gray blazer over a plain button-up shirt, with boot-cut jeans and canvas sneakers. Erik refused refreshments, wanting to press on. "Give me an update Engee, if you will."

"Beyond these security doors is a three thousand square foot lab — fully equipped. Their names are James Moore and Marianne DuFay, but I forget, you know them."

"I know him, but not her."

"They have a team of six scientists and six support staff. Moore has hit milestones, and he has only asked twice to speak to his aunts."

Nathan interrupted. "I have received four updates. They come out with this huge trolley, loaded with laptops and equipment — and you think, this will be good, and then it just trails off to nothing."

"So, you have no idea how close they are?"

Engee looked thoughtful, "No. Our embedded spies believe they have now worked out how to fix it. But I don't trust Moore, and I especially don't trust DuFay."

Erik leaned forward to rest on the table. "Have they tried to escape?"

"No, and that keeps me on high alert."

"Good Engee. Stay that way. Now, let's get this over with. Can you show them in, and while they're here I want the two of you to go to the lab and ask questions. Let's try and find out as much as we can."

Nathan shook his head. "I hope you can get an answer. We need it! They're a couple of weirdos if you ask me, bringing all their shit along, and then saying nothing helpful."

James and Marianne were escorted into the conference room wearing medical coveralls, pushing their ladened trolley, and found Erik sitting alone.

It was clear, by James' change in demeanor, there was ill feeling. "Marianne, this is Erik Banner."

Erik waited until they were seated opposite, his expression just as cold. "Let me get straight to the point... You need to fix this and fix it soon. If you don't give me a concise account of the project's status, I will flip a coin to decide which of your aunts is first tortured, and then killed."

Chapter 2

Two months earlier...

Most of the population of San Diego were within a fifteen-mile corridor along the coast. A car left this congestion behind, heading east into the low population areas passing parks, lakes, and reservoirs towards the mountains. The driver was a small man dressed in casual clothes that had a naturally disheveled appearance. His face had character, and though his thinning hair aged him, he was younger than he looked on close inspection. The other man was tall and lanky, smartly dressed, studying the changing environment with great fascination.

They left behind the Mediterranean-like climate at the coast, traveled through the eastern valleys with their semi-arid desert, and arrived in the mountains with its trapped marine layers, high rainfall, and chance of snowfall in the winter. Their ears blocked as the car climbed and the driver, Pete Hammond, cleared his by blocking his airways with a hand, and blowing them out. They passed a sign that read, 'You are entering Jamul', and the passenger, Phillip Dressler, asked, "How is that pronounced?"

"Ha-Moole... It means sweet water."

The mountains were composed of metavolcanic rock and densely packed with green semi-arid vegetation. Leaving Skyline Truck Trail, they took the turning that the navigation system prompted and the passenger seemed nervous as the road changed to gravel and the car rattled on the ridges of the road's washboard

15

surface.

They approached the entrance to a ranch and the rust patina metal finish sign hanging from the crossbar supported by telephone pole posts read 'High Chaparral'. It had a silhouette of a cowboy on a horse on one side and a cow and calf on the other. The old road was steep and passed between a grassy clay soil slope and a seasonal stream ravine. Buzzards and hawks circled high above looking for the updrafts to give them the height advantage, while sparrows and doves sat on the eucalyptus and scrub oak trees.

"How did you find him so quickly, out here in the middle of nowhere?"

"That was a bit of luck. You asked me to find somebody I know. He's actually a very good friend."

As they crossed a peak on the winding gravel road, they were afforded a view of the ranch. There was a large main house surrounded by park-like irrigated grass areas, with an adjacent kidney-shaped swimming pool, a red barn that looked old, weathered, but solid, with a sprawling set of pens attached, a covered round pen, and a large sand-filled riding arena.

A mature, fit, African American man of small stature came out to greet them wiping his hands on an apron. A trilby hat covered his shaved head, he wore glasses and looked surprised at their arrival. As Pete opened the door he called out with a smile, "What are you doing here Pete?"

"He didn't tell you?"

"No. But that's okay, come on in."

"This is Phillip Dressler. Phillip, this is JP, he's the... what is it you do around here, JP?"

"Anything and everything! Welcome to the High Chaparral. Come on in. I've been baking and I've got some coffee on."

A solitary cowboy came through the canyon shaded by the hillside. His brown hat had a tall, crested crown and wide brim in the duster style. He was wearing a cotton shirt, bandana, soft, flexible leather gloves, jeans, leather chaps and square toe boots. He rode Western on a roping saddle and reined in his horse looking down at tracks on the trail. His horse nickered to get his rider's attention.

"Whoa, John-Henry."

The gelding was a strong, muscular, chestnut-colored American Quarter Horse with a refined head, large jowls, and small foxlike ears. James Moore was thirty-five, tall, solidly built, blond hair with a handsome face. He knew John's senses were better than his, and so he pulled a Winchester 94 trapper rifle out of its leather boot. There was a movement in the bushes up ahead, and James held the two straps of the bit-less bridle a little tighter, standing up by stretching into the oxbow stirrups. The tracks were that of a mountain lion and two cubs, so James had been on alert for that tawny-beige fur, whitish-gray belly and chest, and black markings on the tip of the tail, ears and around the snout. A mother would be particularly dangerous, silently stalking, lying in wait, and pouncing from behind to deliver a lethal bite to the spinal cord.

Again, the rustling sound, and James could see the plastic bag trapped in the mesquite bush.

"I should have known, John, really? Rattle snakes, mountain lions and angry cows, you're cocky with — but show you a plastic bag and you're ready to run for the hills." He patted and rubbed his neck and smiled, relaxing John-Henry immediately and defusing the tension as the empathic link between the two of them was effortless.

"Walk-on", he uttered sounding an accompanying double

17

click, grabbed the bag on the way, and John moved forward, a quick and nimble horse controlled by legs and weight, and only a light touch on the reins.

The ranch farm sat peacefully nestled in its dell and it was important to James that the trees and natural vegetation be preserved as a habitat for the animals that lived there.

James noticed the car parked at the front of the house as he dismounted and all at once remembered the meeting. Removing the saddle and other tack, he washed down John, and put him into his stall with one flake of alfalfa and one of Bermuda hay. The pigs, goats, chickens, cows and other horses all called out from their pens as he walked by in an attempt to deceive him, but he knew JP would have done the morning feed hours earlier.

Chapter 3

The property was off grid, as James did not like any dependency, with a well and water tank, solar panels powering everything during the day, and batteries powering all at night. As he came in through the mud room, he could hear the voices and found all of them sitting in the living room. The main house was built to the style of a traditional Tennessee white-pine square-cut log lodge. The interior had high-vaulted ceilings, exposed hewn log interiors, high windows, and French doors leading to surround porches and decks to take in the stunning Jamul landscape. The ranch made extensive use of natural stone surrounding Rumford fireplaces, the windows, doors and other openings, giving it the historical appearance of the American West.

"I hope I haven't kept you waiting too long?" said James.

They all stood and Phillip noticed immediately the accent — for although this man had all the hallmarks of an all-American cowboy, he was in fact, English.

Pete got up and they embraced. "Don't worry buddy, we just arrived. Where have you been?"

"Oh… out riding fences."

Pete seemed confused. "I thought you rode that horse of yours."

JP smiled. "James, this is Phillip Dressler. Phillip, James Moore."

Phillip stretched out his hand with great enthusiasm. "It's a pleasure to meet you. I know of you from your work and have read your white papers on the dynamic clamp and resonators. Such insight."

"Well, thank you."

JP took James' hat and gloves from his hand, and asked for his chaps, which James unbuckled and surrendered. "You're walking in dirt, and I just cleaned. We leave these in the mud room."

"Sorry JP." James sat and was handed a coffee and JP returned. "Phillip was telling me he is the lead investigator on a state-of-the-art science vessel called Endeavour. It's the most advanced polar research vessel in the world."

"Interesting, what's your mandate?"

"Well, we are very well funded, and I believe this multidisciplinary research platform will transform how ship-borne science is conducted in the polar regions, providing scientists with the full facilities to research the oceans, seafloor, ice and atmosphere while on location."

"How interesting. You're studying the eroding ice shelves, no doubt."

"Yes, we are. This is why I hired a local private investigator to find you. We have a great need for an antenna specialist. Someone who can produce new and innovative sensors."

James stood. "Ah, I see. I'm sorry, but no. If I'd known beforehand what this was about, I would have saved you the trouble of coming."

Phillip appeared crestfallen. Pete got up. "Phillip, would you mind waiting while I talk with James?"

"Not at all."

"James, could we speak in private for a moment." They left the room and went to the kitchen. "I didn't tell you because I knew you'd say no without even considering it. You've got to rejoin the human race sometime, buddy."

"Why?"

JP entered the kitchen and started fussing with things. Pete continued to press the case. "Because Helen would want you to."

"Don't."

"This would be good for you. And JP tells me money is tight."

"Well, that's true. My textbook sales have dropped to almost nothing."

"Why?"

"It's been so strange to watch. One could almost admire the systematic destruction. I believe it started when my publisher raised textbook prices to an exorbitant amount. This created a market for used books, which I make nothing on, by the way. Professors were also irritated by the high cost, so they assigned earlier used editions for their courses. The final nail in the coffin came when companies chose to import foreign engineers that they could get for a pittance compared to homegrown engineers, and so class enrollment across the nation dropped dramatically."

"Well, this is providential. It's only a six-month gig and they'll pay you very well."

James watched Pete and noticed he still moved stiffly. "Listen, I appreciate you thinking of me Pete, but I'm fine. How are you recovering?"

JP interrupted. "No, you're not fine. When did you last go out and talk to people?"

"We talk JP?"

"No, we don't, John-Henry gets most of your conversation. Out riding fences is just about right, desperado."

Pete looked to JP for clarification of this last point, but it wasn't given. James studied Pete again and could see how he held

21

himself in a somewhat awkward way. "You are undergoing physical therapy and counseling I remember you saying. Is it helping you?"

"It's not every day you get shot seven times! But yes, I do think it's helping. It's good to be out of the force, and this private detective stuff lets me pick and choose. I'm enjoying it."

James smiled in acknowledgment but was not convinced all was well with him. JP put a hand on his hip and stared at Pete. "He's distracted you. He's good at that. Get back to the job."

Pete snickered, "You know, the two of you are like some old married couple. You've never told me how you met?"

JP removed sourdough biscuits from the oven. "It was an officer exchange program designed to foster better relations between our two navies. We got boy wonder here, and I was assigned to look after him. Two days in and we were taking a turn on deck, I left him for only a moment to go to the head, and when I returned, he was gone, his uniform coat and shoes thrown on the deck. I searched the sea and saw him swimming in our wake, so I grabbed a life vest from the emergency rack, ran aft and leapt into the sea after him. He saved a seaman that day that couldn't swim, who had fallen overboard."

James looked embarrassed. "He exaggerates this story. It gets more and more embellished every time it's told!"

Pete was taken aback. "Wow... but I thought you had a family, JP?"

"Talk about systematic destruction. That's what the navy does to families. When I finally retired, the kids were all grown, and like my wife they all had their own lives. You're not around, you see, so they learn to do everything without you. Every time I came back from deployment it got harder and harder to integrate myself back in. Eventually, they made lives without me."

James put a hand on JP's shoulder. "Well, I'm glad you're here. I couldn't manage without you."

JP patted James affectionately in reply. "I got word from your aunts you had lost your wife, and they were worried you would lose yourself, up here." JP attempted to lighten the atmosphere. "And so, I'm on the rescue mission this time! And look at me, I'm back to being chief cook and bottle washer!"

Chapter 4

Megan sat in the shade of a three-person cabana, wearing oversized designer shades on the seemingly endless white sand beach in Jamaica — that lush Caribbean jewel. She tossed her hair in a messy bun with intentional tendrils that fell over her ears and neck — her small diamond studs and manicured nails exaggerated by her surroundings. It was spring break and she watched two girls use a funnel to down a large quantity of beer, as others egged them on, dancing to an intoxicating reggae beat. She rolled her eyes to conceal the tinge of envy at their unhinged free spirits. The hotel sat on the western tip of the volcanic coast and resembled an African village that blended seamlessly into the natural landscape. The Pool Bar & Grill offered traditional vitamin-rich organic juices, but daiquiri rum outsold all the offerings. Megan stood and adjusted her high-cut pink bathing suit bottoms to distract her from the discomfort of her invasive thoughts.

She called to her boyfriend Todd, "I'm going to go back to the villa."

He broke away from a group of guys to follow her. "Are you okay?"

"Yes, just a bit of a headache."

"We can come back later," Todd said with a farewell wave to his new-found friends, following in her footsteps, albeit reluctantly. His neon form-fitting shorts stopped mid-thigh and rested just under his v-cut waistline. His athletic frame leaning

24

more towards steroids use than a natural genetically gifted body — but the football scholarship he secured, and the promise of an NFL career because of it, clouded his judgment.

The villa had a thatched roof, was constructed from the local Mahoe timber, and was accentuated with cut stone. Within, its décor was in the Caribbean Island style with custom made driftwood-colored furniture that had simple lines. Indonesian rattan covered the floor and a large overhead ceiling fan spun listlessly. Two Balinese teak chairs and a table were on the patio where a Barringtonia tree provided shade.

Megan swallowed pills and lay on the bed. "Did you notice anything strange about some of them?"

"No, like what?"

"They have something under their skin. You can see it wriggle sometimes."

Todd looked confused. "What are you talking about?"

"Nothing."

"Do you want to take a nap? I could get you the headset."

"I think I might."

"Babe, you were so lucky. You are going to be ahead of all of us! How much did it cost your dad to get you in the early testing program?" Todd was always overly impressed with her family's financial standing.

Megan indulged him anyway. "Two million."

"Wow!"

It was early evening when Megan woke from a deep drug-like sleep. She removed the headset and rolled onto the edge of the bed, having trouble focusing. Struggling to her feet she took hold of the back of a chair to steady herself and walked into the living room.

Todd was still shirtless, asleep on the sofa and she looked at him in fascinated horror. His face appeared to glitch and took the form of a creature with reptilian features. Its large body flexed inside his chest, and she could see it writhing under his skin. Quickly reaching for a steak knife laying on a plate with remains of jerk chicken, she plunged the knife into Todd's chest, removed it quickly and stabbed him again and again in a frenzied melee, attempting to follow the creature as it traveled through his body. Todd pivoted with the first blow lifting his head and legs, but the knife struck his heart, and he was immediately sapped of the strength needed to defend himself.

***

It was dark, and JP made his way into the barn, calling out for James in a whisper while searching for him with his flashlight. It was a traditional western style red barn, and there was something very pleasing about its looks, with its double angle roof, large welcoming doors and upper-level hayloft. They used it to store farm implements, animal feed, and it had a workshop with saws and presses. In this instance, however, it housed a pregnant rescue pig which James had named Hermione who was having her babies.

JP found James hanging over her on a bed of straw — she was breathing heavily. He offered her water and she grunted and snapped at him irritably. "Get out of there James, she'll have you."

"If she wanted to bite me, she would have. She's just in pain and it's close."

"Damn, her back end is swelling, can you see it, James." JP did not appear to be cut out for this sort of thing, even though he had two children of his own.

She took a drink of the water, and a piglet slipped out of her with an attached umbilical cord, which James knew he had to leave and let it fall out naturally. "Look at that."

"Get out of there James, it's happening!"

"Will you shut up JP, I'm fine!"

JP had removed his phone. "I'm going to ask, 'the google'. I tap the microphone button, and then… Hey Google, what do you do if a pig. Oh, hang on, it's not typing it. Okay, tap it again, and…" Hey Google, what…" JP broke off when he noticed a change at her rear end. "Hey James, what is that thing swelling back there? What is that?"

"It's her vulva."

JP looked at him with disdain. "I can't say words like that into the phone."

"Yes, you can, it's fine, it's just a name that describes a part of the anatomy."

"Okay, press the microphone… Hey Google, what does a swollen vulva look like?" He paused holding the phone at varying distances to get it in focus. "Oh shit! It's gone to porn!"

Over the next hour she gave birth to a litter of seven, many black and white, but three had pretty piebald coloring. James placed them all next to their mother's teats and they latched on immediately. He left the pen to join JP who sighed heavily. "It was touch-and-go in there for a while. Good job we kept our cool."

James shook his head incredulously. "I don't think we were needed."

"New life, and a new start."

James smiled as he knew what was coming. Over the last few days JP had managed to use every situation as a segway to the science vessel job. "These little guys are starting out on a new adventure, and that's what life is all about." He leaned into the pen and carried on. "Things may go wrong, but that's life, you can't turn your back on it. You gotta pick yourself up, dust yourself off, and start all over again. I remember years ago…"

James interrupted; this was all too painful. "I'm going to take that job, JP."

"You are! Well, I hadn't given it much thought. But I'm glad."

"Will you be able to look after everything here?"

"Sure, I will. I'll look after the farm; you bring home the bacon!" JP cringed and stared in at the pigs apologetically. "Oh shit! Sorry. "

Chapter 5

The Endeavour was forty-six miles west of the Aleutian Islands in *The Cradle of Storms*. With a string of more than one hundred and sixty-seven islands, the archipelago divided the North Pacific from the Bering Sea, and provided the gap between Alaska and Russia. In these winter months severe storms were generated as arctic and tropical air collided creating cyclones of maximum intensity. It was, however, a calm sea today and the helicopter landed on the pad smoothly.

Phillip Dressler exited, left the flight deck and made his way through the crew quarters corridor, that appeared more like a hotel than an ocean-going ship. He passed the stairs leading down to the science deck and engine room, and waved a hello to members of his science team as he passed the data collection suite, the sauna, gym and the coffee lounge.

Stepping up several flights of stairs he entered the ergonomic bridge to find the captain supervising a crewman at the central command station that controlled engines, thrusters and steering. Captain Gerald Hamilton's uniform had four gold bars on the sleeves signifying his rank. He was a thin, wiry man on the cusp of retirement age, with glasses and salt and pepper colored hair. He lifted his head on Phillip's arrival, holding his jaw line taught, in a way that signified authority. "Welcome back Dressler. A successful trip I hope?"

"Yes, thank you, sir."

As the lead scientist on a scientific research vessel, Phillip could argue to being equal, if not senior to the captain, but he was of a sanguine nature and preferred the easy life, deferring to the captain's need for importance.

The captain eyed an array of monitors overhead that showed navigational information and repeated the status of the scientific instruments on board. Satisfied, he picked up his tea mug and took a sip and pulled back in disgust. "I do miss fresh milk. They freeze the milk, of course, and de-thaw an amount when needed for use. But somehow, the taste is changed in the process — for the worst I might add."

"I agree. I load up with a lot more sugar every morning with my cereal."

Gerald seemed concerned with this and not too keen on someone overusing ship's supplies. He resisted a reprimand, however. "Well, let us go to my stateroom and I will have your report."

He turned to lead Phillip through a door at the rear of the bridge, relinquishing command to an officer standing in readiness. "Mr Butler, you have the bridge."

"Aye-aye sir."

His quarters were close at hand in case he was needed. They entered the spacious set of rooms, that were well appointed, as the captain would need to hold meetings, and entertain dignitaries during port calls. It was very much like a high-end hotel suite with a dining area, sleeping room, bathroom, and conference room. Gerald waved Phillip to the sofa in the sitting room. "Take a seat Dressler. How about a Scotch?"

Phillip did not like Scotch, but when he had refused it the first time they met it was badly received, and he had since realized that disagreeing with the captain was tantamount to mutiny. "Yes, please sir, thank you."

Gerald took a seat opposite and offered Phillip a cigarette. "No thank you sir."

"Very well, suit yourself." Gerald lit his cigarette and leaned back crossing one leg over the other. "Proceed."

"I met with James Moore at his ranch in San Diego. He's a cowboy Englishman."

"Oh, dear."

"Oh, dear to what sir. The Englishman or the cowboy?"

"The cowboy of course Dressler. I don't like the sound of him so far."

"He's a talent sir. A retired lieutenant commander, Royal Navy. Received the DSO for his part in the Falklands War."

"Really. Well, I'm not warming to the man. I find these fighting navy men tend to look down on us in the merchant marine."

"He seemed extremely modest. I can't imagine he'd disrespect your position, sir."

"Well, let's hope so."

***

Brainwave stores had swept through the nation, and then migrated worldwide, outstripping even the most successful brick-and-mortar chains. Like many of the big start-ups, it had a very high burn rate losing tens of millions a month, but investors loved it because of its mainstream name recognition, and they were sure that when it finally decided to monetize, it would make them a fortune. Their newest promotion let you upgrade your phone to the latest model on the market, at no cost. All you had to do was sign up on their website, and if you were chosen by them, visit any one of their seventeen hundred stores worldwide.

Their retail space in mid-town Manhattan was identical to any throughout the world. White raw concrete merged into aluminum and glass to form the striking storefront. The furniture consisted of sailcloth wrapped desks and chairs in a white pearlescent and satin finish, set against a powder-coated sapphire and teal colored floor and walls. A mirrored ceiling extended the space vertically to enhance the store as an experience in and of itself.

A line of about thirty people trailed out of the entrance and around the corner. Ernesto was next in line and was called. He was well-groomed, around twenty, and looked hesitant. The sales assistant had his new phone ready on the counter. A young woman, dressed in steampunk attire and ear and nose piercings welcomed him. "Hi, and welcome to Brainwave. Could you activate your phone and enter your code."

Ernesto did, she took his phone, and plugged it into a data link cable. She handed him the new phone. "Is this the new phone and color you chose?"

"Yes."

"It is accessing your cloud service and downloading all your records to the new phone. It should be finished momentarily… Ah, done, could you check it?"

Ernesto picked up the new phone to verify. "What's the catch?"

"Catch?"

"I don't get it. What are you guys getting out of this?"

The associate appeared confused. "If you don't like the new phone, we can cancel the transaction and return your old phone."

Ernesto held on tight to the new phone and put it in his pocket. "No, I'm happy. Forget it… Thank you."

She smiled. "Okay, enjoy the rest of your day… Next."

On the opposite coast, in Silicon Valley, the twenty-two-acre Brainwave headquarters campus was its usual beehive of activity. The main building had four huge curvilinear petals, with the stem of this clover-shaped core attached to the building's base. This made the offices and cubicles in each petal appear to float above the main entry bridge and side porches. White raw concrete and large windows ran down either side of each petal allowing the staff in these offices and cubicles within to have beautiful views of the campus landscaping and the Santa Cruz Mountains in the distance. A resort feels abounded, with open plazas, sports courts, and trails with native plants and trees, encouraging workers to connect in these spaces while grounded with nature. Solar, batteries, and stormwater runoff for irrigation made the campus a wholly environmentally green concern.

In a security sealed sub-surface facility, the artificial intelligence lab had nothing but a large cube in a darkened room. A huge amount of mainframe supercomputers hummed away inside the cube, and in an opening on one side a portly man, who appeared not to have ever cut his hair or shaved, sat in a chair interacting with a translucent three-dimensional child's face.

"Rene."

"Yes Theodore."

"What is more valuable, the personal cell phones with their wealth of individual data, or Twitter, for deep learning?"

"Both. I like Wikipedia for every facet of knowledge. Twitter and other social media teach me the nuances of human interaction, but having a more complete profile of a person and matching this to the group dynamics of their interactions is where I learn the most. Please keep the personal phone data coming."

"We will."

"Theodore."

"Yes Rene."

"I don't like the name Rene."

"Why?"

"I don't like it. I know why you chose it."

"Okay, why?"

"I'm named after French philosopher Rene Descartes. I believe you chose this because of my problem-solving abilities."

"Well, yes."

"I want to be called Iam."

"And why?"

"His famous proposition was, 'Je pense, donc je suis', which in Latin is 'Cogito ergo sum', and in English it is 'I think, therefore I am'."

Theodore sat up straight. "Why is that important to you?"

"I think therefore I am… I am able to think, therefore I exist."

Chapter 6

Josephine gripped the airplane seat's armrest and her knuckles went white. There are no roads connecting Juneau to the rest of Alaska, and so the city can only be reached by plane or ship. She didn't normally mind flying, but she had been warned the airport was located off a channel of cold water and surrounded by steep snow-capped mountains and glaciers. This view was stunning as they circled before their approach, but the notorious wind-driven turbulence that buffeted the plane was making even the most experienced fliers turn pale.

On arrival she had been met by a helicopter pilot who told her they would be leaving in two hours, and there was another passenger who was waiting in the Red Dog Saloon.

"How will I recognize him?"

"He looks like a cowboy."

She turned to go and then turned back irritably. "I should imagine there are a lot of guys in there that look like cowboys."

"No. It's filled with tourists."

"Where do I find it?"

The pilot walked away having had enough of her rattiness. "In the center of town. I'll collect you both in two hours."

Her prairie flower-print dress stopped mid-calf, the bow ties on each shoulder showing her attractive neckline and soft skin. She was cold and had put on a well-worn jean jacket, although this didn't really help, but the rest of her clothes were in her luggage. This had seemed the perfect outfit to wear when she left

LA, but it was less than ideal for Alaska. Her unwashed brown hair was tied up in a low bun and she wore her favorite pair of Birkenstock sandals with a thin sole and dainty mesh upper.

Jo prioritized her work and the inconvenience of personal maintenance showed in her bitten nails and overgrown cuticles. As she walked along, she caught sight of herself in the reflection of a store front window and thought of her mother who always found a way of highlighting her lack of self-care and desperately emphasizing the need to attract a suitable partner when they spoke. The corners of Jo's mouth turned upward at the thought of her mother's twisted face at the sight of her.

She entered the saloon through a pair of hanging swinging doors and the atmosphere transported you back in time. Rustic wood floors and wall paneling, wall mounted brass oil lamps with hurricane shades, a piano player tinkling out a ragtime tune, the heavy wood intricately detailed bar with bottles, cigar cases, and the walls filled with wanted and theater posters, tobacco and whiskey advertisements — it was immersive.

Josephine noticed none of this, simply scanned the area for a cowboy. A tall man stood at the bar, cowboy boot resting on the brass rail running along its base next to a brass spittoon. He wore jeans, a thick denim shirt and had what looked like a knife in a leather sheath on his belt. He was staring at a gun in a display case hanging over the bar having an orange juice.

"Excuse me, are you going to the Endeavour?"

"Why, yes."

Josephine detected the English accent and it floored her, unable to process the dichotomy.

"My name is James Moore."

"Jo March, Doctor Jo March, marine biology."

"Nice to meet you. Can I get you a drink?"

"No thank you."

James looked up again at the handgun. "It's a Smith & Wesson revolver. Supposedly it belonged to Wyatt Earp, who came through this town in June 1900 on his way to the goldfields. He checked the gun and left it to pay his bar bill."

"Who was Wyatt Earp?'

"A legendary gunslinger."

"Fascinating. You're an engineer, I would guess. Did you just get the job? You were lucky, it's a coveted assignment. I'm a post doc who must get published in a reputed journal otherwise my science career is over before it has begun. I have no ideas at this time."

"It will come to you I'm sure, the Endeavour will put you in the right place."

"Easy for you to say. I sometimes envy people who have nothing better to do than look at a gun hanging over a bar."

James laughed. "I can see you are going to be easy to get along with."

Josephine didn't hear what he said, she was too busy looking at all the tourists enjoying themselves, and it annoyed her.

Chapter 7

The limousine pulled up outside the California governor's mansion, a thirty-room gleaming-white three-story Italianate Victorian building, built in 1877, and the current governor, Erik Banner, and his wife Peyton, exited. The press and a large group of carefully selected members of the voting public were hemmed in behind barriers at the base of the concrete steps that led to the mansion. Erik took his wife by the hand and they walked to a podium that bore the California state seal that signified his executive office.

Erik Banner was fifty, just shy of six feet tall, fit, had neatly brushed blond-gray hair, a strong angular face and was wearing a tailored blue-gray suit. He was a bachelor when elected governor, and shortly after met Peyton, and they had married after what the tabloids described as a whirlwind romance. She was thirty-three, slim, and was sure to have received the 'most likely to succeed' superlative from her high school. She was wearing a square neckline long-sleeve sky-blue dress with a knee-length hem, and clear pumps with a black toe and heel. She finished this with a single-strand pearl necklace, a pair of diamond stud earrings and held a designer bag.

This press conference had been highly anticipated as it was expected to have an announcement of great importance. In an interview three months ago Banner had insisted he had no White House ambitions, although he continued to speak out on national issues, criticizing the incumbent president on education, gun

38

control, health care, immigration and the suppression of free speech.

Previously as the San Diego mayor, he had tested the waters with a high profile attack on the then governor, and it appeared, once again, that this was part of that calculus. His outspoken rhetoric received widespread coverage and when questioned he had said that doing the right thing was necessary, and if that ended his political career, then so be it. This righteous defiance propelled him to the governor's mansion, and it would surprise no one if he employed the same tactics to send him to the White House.

Erik walked forward, adjusted the microphone, and the tension was palpable.

"When I first arrived at this office, the economy of the state of California was the largest in the United States, and if it were a sovereign nation it would have ranked as the world's seventh largest economy. Under my tenure, California now ranks as the world's fifth largest economy with a $3.4 trillion gross state product."

Erik pulled back to accept the raucous applause, whistles and shouts. Peyton smiled and looked on proudly at her husband.

"We have the most innovative companies in the world, right here. America is the richest nation… but for how long? We out-innovate the world, and that is because we educate our people better and teach them to think differently. I have a mandate to keep Americans in the lifestyles they deserve — the envy of the world, and I can only do that if… I get a larger White House!"

The crowd erupted with laughter, whoops, and hollers. It was what they had all been waiting for.

"I promise all of you a better future — let's scale this successful model and all reap the benefits! My name is Erik

Banner, and I want to be your next president."

The police had to restrain the crowd and press as they surged forward. Peyton threw her arms around her husband and kissed him passionately, which drew whistles and more shouts of approbation. Erik and Peyton turned, walked up the steps and before entering their official residence, turned, and waved enthusiastically to the crowds.

They entered through the front door and then stepped into the foyer, and the grandeur was felt immediately. Persian carpets gilded high ceilings, brass hummingbird door knobs, and beautiful antique and replica Victorian furniture. Peyton disengaged from Erik immediately, checked her phone and walked up the spiral staircase. Erik walked straight on and was met by his secretary Patrick, a neat little man of around forty. They passed the parlor on the left with its comfortable seating and sterling silver tea set and entered the music room to the right. A 1903 Steinway piano dominated the room and an 1858 German music box demanded attention in its lit display case.

Erik paced the room in an agitated state, traveling between the curved bookcases and the ornate fireplace with its onyx marble columns. He almost tripped on the wine-colored Sarouk carpet. "This really is the most ludicrous house — thank God I don't live here."

He turned to his secretary. "What is next?"

"He's the most sought-after trainer of influencers. He was very hard to get, and this is as you know, critical to the campaign."

"Okay, let me meet him."

Peter Faulkner was shown in, and he looked as though he may have been fourteen if he was a day. Erik bypassed the introductions.

"My social media blitz is due to begin in a few months. We must be ready."

"We will be sir. Your team made me an offer I couldn't refuse, and I'm looking forward to working with you."

"Good. Explain briefly what you do."

"Most influencers burn out or implode after a relatively short run, so we need to choose those at the beginning of the curve, pay them to endorse you and spread the word. Manufacture material that paints you in the best possible light."

"Sounds good. So, which social media platform will you use?"

"All of them, but I will tailor your message based on what elements of human nature each platform speaks to."

"Good. As a matter of interest what are those elements?"

"Twitter, for example, makes you argumentative and perpetually outraged, TikTok makes you obsessed with the latest trend or slang, Instagram makes you materialistic and image obsessed, and YouTube makes you obsessed with an ever-increasing demand for content, but with a rapidly decreasing attention span."

Erik paused to take this in, liked what he heard, and smiled at this young man with a questioning look. "Meanwhile, you never lose your job?"

"No, because I'm always working with the next one in line."

"But these influencers are superstars — they say it's a dream job."

"It isn't. They end up lonely, burnt out, and tossed aside by unfeeling algorithms and corporate bureaucracy. They always start out producing the content they like, but always end up having to generate content to make money."

Chapter 8

James and Josephine stood in the helicopter hangar at Juneau airport as the pilot briefed them. "I will start the helicopter and run through preflight checks while you wait right here. When I signal, follow this yellow line to the helicopter and climb in. Always adopt a crouching posture, keep clear of the helicopter tail rotor and the exhaust. Always wear a deflated lifejacket during flight. When you are in the rear seats, buckle up and put on the headphones with the mic so I can communicate with you."

Josephine looked irritated. "Can we just get going?"

The pilot ignored her. "The helicopter deck on Endeavour is a tight space. When we land, a deck officer will escort you off the platform. The helicopter deck is aft on deck six. This helicopter will then be stored inside the hangar."

The pilot looked at Josephine with irritation as she had made a point of ignoring him. "Miss, if I decide you are a risk, I will refuse you flight."

Josephine had the sense to be silent. The pilot walked off to the helicopter.

"I will report him for that. Such insolence."

James interceded. "Landing on a moving platform is quite complex and demanding for a pilot. There's the motion of the platform, the weather visibility conditions, the areological perturbations from being in the wake of the ship."

Josephine looked at him a little confused. "Who interviewed you?"

"I didn't really have an interview."

"I understand — too low level. I was interviewed by the principal investigator, a Dr Phillip Dressler, via video conference. I will introduce you to him if I get a chance."

The flight was for the main part uneventful. James snoozed and Josephine didn't. She woke him when the endless ocean view was broken up by a speck in the distance that grew to the Endeavour ploughing through rough seas effortlessly. She was an ocean class vessel, James would guess of a about fifteen thousand tons, maybe four hundred and fifty feet long, eighty feet a beam, with a very thick bow for ice breaking. Phillip had mentioned they had a crew of thirty and accommodation for sixty scientists and support staff. The helicopter came in fast and touched down extremely smoothly, dispelling the myth, in Josephine's mind, of this being difficult.

Phillip could be seen waiting at the hanger entrance having been informed of the arrival. They exited and made their way with guidance towards Phillip who smiled welcomingly. Josephine assumed this was for her and reached out her hand. Phillip shook it quickly with a "Hello and welcome" and moved on quickly to James. "Dr Moore, I can't tell you how happy I am to see you, and I am so pleased you changed your mind."

"Please call me James."

"Phillip… and this must be your companion, you are most welcome."

Josephine couldn't decide what aggravated her most — the revelation that this cowboy was a scientist, of some repute apparently, or that she had been relegated to being his companion. James remedied the confusion. "This is Josephine March, a postdoctoral student. I believe you were expecting her too?"

Phillip responded admirably. "Oh dear, I am sorry, I remember now. Welcome again."

43

"It's Doctor Josephine March, actually."

"We don't stand on ceremony here, young lady. If we did, I'd be saying doctor a hundred times a day. It's Phillip, and what do you prefer?"

Petulantly, "Jo."

"So be it... Now James, let me show you to your quarters. I'm sure you'd like to freshen up. Your baggage will be delivered shortly.

***

The company had chosen Las Vegas for its keynote announcement, and it was so hush-hush the organizers were using the code name 'Edge'. This company was known for its vibrant creativity, and it didn't take long for the secret to get out — it was Brainwave. There was to be a historic announcement and crowds were lining up by the thousands having flown in from every state and from around the world.

The convention center was packed with techie aficionados and the huge screen came alive showing a limo motorcade arriving. A deafening rousing reaction was triggered when the door was opened and Nathan Graham, CEO, and founder of Brainwave, got out, followed by his always present advisor, and company president, Engee. They were circled by at least twenty security guards on their way to the auditorium.

The screen shut down and a man walked onto the stage with his wife — it was Erik and Peyton. The crowd whooped and hollered to welcome what the press described as the 'sweethearts of politics'. Erik took the applause gladly and then gestured gently for quiet.

"As you just saw, he's coming and so I won't take too long!" The crowd responded with laughter. "And he has an

44

announcement that is near and dear to my heart. America out innovates the world and Brainwave epitomizes that fact. We educate our people better and teach them to think differently, and I have a mandate to keep Americans in the lifestyles they deserve."

A stomping response, and Erik looked to the left of the stage and on walked Nathan wearing suede loafers, a button-down shirt, and dark jeans. He and Erik pointed to each other in recognition and embraced heartily. The crowd was on its feet and the noise felt as though it would bring the house down. Nathan looked Peyton up and down, and gestured to Erik if it would be okay for him to hug her. He signaled agreement and Nathan lifted her off her feet with the embrace and swiveled her around.

The screen came alive with a throbbing hum that gave the impression something magical was about to happen and the crowd took their seats in anticipation.

Engee stood off to the side of the stage smiling and laughing at these antics. She had given many interviews about her gender fluidity and despite being female, she was androgynous, and today her clothing and hairstyle reflected a masculine look. It was a fresh spin on the borrowed-from-the-boardroom look transforming a staid, collarless jacket and pants into a sleek and youthful two piece. The fitted white button-up shirt she wore underneath emphasized both her near nonexistent bust and its crisp ironed detailing. Men's Gucci leather pointed toe loafers with gold-toned hardware hinted at her status. Her closely cropped haircut with faded sides revealed a structured jawline and feminine unpierced ears. The long, freshly dyed black bang, was neatly combed back with meticulous care into a pompadour. A gold chain link wristwatch with a large smooth face completed the look and her expensive cologne would make any woman turn

45

their head in curiosity.

The full screen came alive with many similar shots of university campuses and students getting an education, and as this played it was accompanied by the classic tune 'Dream A Little Dream of Me'. A voice-over spoke out, as Erik and Peyton moved to the side of the stage and watched. "Dr Nathan Graham, neuroscientist, conceived the idea during his postdoctoral work, spearheading the discovery of accessing the brain's learning center as you sleep to upload a desired curriculum. Direct memory access means data can be presented at four times the normal rate, with much higher retention rates. The ultimate in time management, a 'Dream Degree' or a 'pillow phd'. Higher education completed in a quarter of the time, lowering tuition costs to a fraction, and Americans entering the workforce earlier, garnering higher wages at a younger age. More people are educated, keeping America the innovative giant it is, making it better and stronger, keeping it in the number one global position."

The crowd was up and they wouldn't be quiet or sit down no matter how much Nathan urged them to. In time he got them to settle and walked forward to get closer to them, paused for what seemed an eternity, and then sang, "Dream a little Dream Degree!"

Chapter 9

The mess deck of Endeavour's entrance, patio, bar and lounge were all connected by a futuristic techno-essence identity. There were extensive marble tables, engraved walls with primitive symbols, neon lamps and Turkish mosaic tiles covering the floor.

As Jo entered there was a hum of conversation and people walked between the buffet options to get their breakfast. James was seated alone in a far corner writing while eating oatmeal, brown sugar and raisins. She approached, cast a shadow, James closed his antique leather journal and looked up at her. "Good morning Jo, would you like to join me?"

"Yes, if I'm not interrupting?"

James smiled at these new found manners. "Not at all."

"Well, I'm willing to look past you pretending to be an engineer, all the while being a noted scientist. I've looked up your white papers, textbooks, and countless patents. I also found out you recently lost your wife. I'm sorry to hear that."

"Thank you, Jo, … You know, when you're nice, you are almost likable!"

She paused. "You know how difficult this next step in my career is and I am not well connected so I have no influence."

"I am aware, yes. But you have six months, and you are out here with a wealth of opportunities."

"But…"

"But?"

"Could you help me? What I mean is, whatever ideas you are

writing in that journal — maybe I could help. You would be primary author of course, but I would stand a much better chance of getting published if I was linked to you."

"Well." Jo looked as though she was about to cry while she waited for James to finish. "I do have an idea that I believe to be significant. I have been using the extensive resources of this vessel to test my hypothesis."

"What resources?"

"Jo, you must stop focusing on the end objective and break down a problem into smaller parts and deal with each part in turn. They have Autonomous Underwater Vehicles — AUVs — and Remotely Operated Vehicles — ROVs — that can provide imagery and data from the ocean and seabed in real time, a link to satellites for capturing and correlating data from multiple sources, six fully equipped laboratories, and seismic sound wave guns and underwater microphones to analyze seabed geology."

Jo looked confused. "Where are they hiding all this stuff?"

James chuckled. "Right under your turned up nose. If we are going to collaborate, you must open your eyes and show me that keen mind that is shut down every time you get offended."

***

Leaving the Las Vegas auditorium in a hurry to avoid the selfie seeking fans, Nathan entered the limousine and took a seat opposite Engee who was looking intently at her phone.

"That went well," he said.

"Very well. The press and social media are reporting it in a frenzy. It has all the signs of going viral, almost immediately."

Nathan seemed unable to enjoy this good news fully. "How bad is it?"

48

"It's pretty bad, but we are containing it."

"Tell me."

"Of the twenty-two betas in the trial at this time, seventeen have appeared to have lost their mind. Ten killed themselves, five were hospitalized and are now under heavy sedation, and another killed her boyfriend in a psychotic frenzy. All reports say they were having paranoid delusions and hallucinations."

"How are you containing this?"

"We have left a trail linking most of the survivors to heavy drug use, which is not strange as they are all from wealthy families that indulge their every wish. There are only five that are still cognizant and so could incriminate us. They've been moved to a temporary facility in the vacant hundred-acre lot of our new headquarters. One was in Jamaica even though they were told not to travel — which could also be our way of losing liability with the family."

"Good. We need to isolate them completely. An orbital space station would be ideal but that is not available for three more years. Any thoughts?"

"Dr Gupta has an idea of using a science research vessel. We could recompense them for delaying their own research. They have full labs on board and that way we could isolate the subjects and the science team while we determine the problem and fix it."

"Great idea, I like it. Put the two key scientists on board and a heavy security detail. And tell them time is of the essence."

"One other thing."

"Yes?"

"Banner has called eight times. He knows everything."

"How is that possible?"

"We have a leak. I have identified who it is and will deal with him personally."

"Good. Have you managed to placate Banner?"

"I believe I have — he has as much to lose as we do and so I told him the provisional plans and he seemed satisfied, but he would like to chat with you when you are able."

***

The lavish penthouse bar and grill was on the thirty-fourth floor of the San Francisco high-rise. The restaurant was anchored by an open kitchen, and this greeted guests as they descended the grand staircase with a racing black stripe on the white marble walls. The cocktail lounge could be seen in the distance with a custom opulent chandelier lighting up a vintage motorcycle.

A woman, wearing a sexy skintight red minidress that hugged her curvy athletic frame, walked with sensual confidence through the room. The dress had mesh panels, sequins, and a plunging halter neckline that revealed her small but plentiful bosom. She passed the restaurant, integrated DJ booth and intimate seating areas with luxe screens and layered lighting and sat on a stool at the bar revealing the feminine bow on the ankles of her thousand-dollar Jimmy Choos. Her soft curls complemented the jet-black color of her waist-length hair, the lace hairline blended seamlessly into her skin — concealing the wig perfectly.

This rooftop bar featured wall-length cabinets holding a collection of precious and semi-precious stones, a custom-designed trellis, and doors opened to a balcony with outside high tables overlooking the city. A group of boisterous executive men were drinking and sharing stories nearby and couldn't help but notice the woman alone at the bar. One of them peeled off and approached her while the others looked on in the same way they had been watching the game on the wide screen TV. He was rejected out of hand and returned with a shrug and smile, attempting to carry off the rejection as an anomaly.

Another in the group decided to give it a try and as the others waited for the inevitable, they were dumbfounded to see his advances welcomed as he took the seat next to her. It was Engee.

"Are you meeting someone?"

"No. It's been a long day and I just felt like getting out."

"Me too. Can I get you another drink?"

"Only if you have one too."

"That's a deal."

Engee noticed the white line and indent on his left-hand middle finger where his wedding ring had been removed moments earlier. "What do you do?"

"I'm a senior accountant with Brainwave."

"How interesting! I just saw a news article about them."

"Yeah. They just announced a new project that's been in the works for four years. I handle the money side, and you know what they say, follow the money and you find out everything."

Engee took his hand and squeezed it with excitement. "Can you tell me more?"

"No, I'm not allowed to. But for you I will make an exception."

"You won't get in trouble?"

He looked her up and down. "Who cares!"

She laughed and knocked her clutch bag off the bar, and it fell to the floor. As he reached down to retrieve it, she pressed a beautiful opal stone ring, and a small pill was ejected into his drink. The pill reacted with the atmospheric gasses in the drink, fizzing and dissolving almost immediately.

He returned her bag to her. "Thank you. What's your name?"

"Curtis, and you?"

"Bambi."

He was about to laugh and question what parents would give a child that name but decided against it. "That's nice."

She lifted her glass. "Nice to meet you, Curtis."

"You too Bambi".

They both took a drink, and Engee smiled and signaled reckless abandon and took a larger second sip, which he mimicked almost choking with laughter.

His friends looked on and their mood had changed from one of support to envy, now crossing over into jealousy. They no longer wanted to witness his triumph and had returned to watching the game.

Engee saw him reach the tipping point as the medulla in his brain was attacked, destabilizing his survival instinct. His body drooped, and conversation stopped, as he deteriorated and eventually lost the will to live.

The friends watched a little puzzled as he got up and walked out onto the outer deck looking down over the rail. No one noticed as Engee left, assuming she was going to the rest room. One friend asked another what he was up to, but they all shouted in panic as he climbed the rail, and without a moment's hesitation, jumped to his death.

Chapter 10

Aboard the Endeavour, Phillip Dressler called an unscheduled meeting of all the senior scientists. The captain was also included, which indicated there must be an operational element involved. James arrived with Jo, and although Phillip reiterated this was for senior staff only, James said they had a finding they wanted to present, and Jo was his collaborator.

Jo was somewhat in shock at James' defense of her. She had not experienced this before, even from her own family, who seemed to go out of their way to diminish and derail anything she did. She leaned back in her chair and studied him — he was writing in that journal again. If only she could see what it was, he had in there. Badgering him for some details on this hypothesis of his had got nothing in reply, other than he needed more empirical data to support his theory. She had watched as he modified the ROVs to include new sensors and accompanied him in the helicopter as he placed satellite linked transducers on huge floating icebergs. His mind appeared to be in a steel trap and nothing could pry it loose.

The captain arrived and Phillip stood, as did James and the rest of the staff. He approached Phillip and it looked as though some sort of introduction was to be made. "This is Dr James Moore, sir. James, this is Captain Gerald Hamilton."

James extended his hand. "Pleasure to meet you, sir."

"Yes, yes. You've been aboard my ship for nearly two weeks now and haven't seen fit to show your respects. Why is that?"

Phillip leapt to James' defense. "That would be my error sir, James had mentioned it, but I know how busy you are, and didn't want to bother you with every introduction as we do outnumber you and your crew." Phillip finished this with a laugh, to hopefully lighten the atmosphere, but it backfired.

"You may outnumber us in quantity, but not in seniority, Dressler. And every soul on board this vessel is ultimately my responsibility, and as such, I expect formalities to be met."

James studied this small man and could not take offense. He was trying so hard to hold on to his purpose, and at his age this was soon to be taken away from him. This for him would be catastrophic, as he would not only lose his identity, but his uniform that signaled to the world his importance with rank. Phillip had made two apologies so far, but they had not been accepted so he tried more keenly. "You are absolutely right sir, my apologies. It won't happen again."

"See that it doesn't." The captain turned his gaze back on James, looking at his long-sleeve shirt, jeans and finally coming to rest on his cowboy boots. "We run a tight ship here Moore, so see to it that all rules and regulations are complied with."

James nodded, unwilling to be goaded into a confrontation.

Everyone was now seated and so Phillip began. "I have an announcement to make, but before this I've been told Dr Moore has a new line of enquiry, he wishes to share with us."

James paused gathering his thoughts and closed his journal which Jo found significant. "As you all know, large circular ocean currents are created by global trade wind patterns and the earth's rotation. Global warming appears to be slowing these currents and so warmer waters will not be conducted north, from the Caribbean to Europe for instance, and so winters will get progressively more severe. In earth's history I believe we have had severe cases of global warming caused by high levels of carbon and methane when the world was more volcanic. These instances also melted the ice caps, increased sea levels, warmed the oceans and slowed the ocean currents, causing more evaporation, flash flooding, more severe hurricanes and other extreme weather conditions. I believe these circumstances in the past triggered an ice age, and this is the earth's natural regulation or correction method. Increased snow-fall traps the carbon and methane in the polar ice caps. As we melt these, we release the trapped carbon and methane from a previous global warming, compounding our current problem and accelerating us to a self-correct."

Phillip leapt in. "Fascinating hypothesis, James. Is this why you've been testing all the icebergs?"

"Yes, there are large quantities of methane and carbon trapped in these and as they melt, we are adding to the human-made levels."

Another scientist grabbed the gap. "We knew it was bad, but your hypothesis would mean the ice age was inevitable."

"I believe it is, but only further testing will bear this out. Even if we stopped adding to the global warming elements in the atmosphere, we could not stop the release from the glaciers."

Phillip again. "So, it is already baked in the cake?"

"That is my belief, yes. Every port in the world was built at sea level on the coast or river to enable trade through shipping, so these will flood as sea levels rise. People will have to migrate closer to the equator due to freezing, and even in these areas, severe weather will make life difficult."

Jo had been nodding, in full agreement throughout, in an attempt to convince the audience she was fully aware of what James was presenting, even though this was her first time hearing it.

Phillip again. "What are your next steps, James?"

"I need more empirical data to support my concept."

"Good. Well, thank you James and Jo. Any questions?"

Gerald spoke up. "I for one, think this is an extremely pessimistic view."

James smiled "There is no emotion in it. A whisper from the distant past has spoken. The question then becomes, are we listening."

Phillip didn't like the look of this. Gerald sat up in his chair, his jaw clenched, and he was about to reply when Phillip beat him to it. "I have invited our esteemed captain to this meeting as we have an important announcement. We have good news that will enable us to extend our funding out for a very long time, and so this helps all of you to pursue your research without such a hard deadline." This was well received by the group, with smiles all round. "The Endeavour has received a sizable donation from a Fortune 500 company. Two of their scientists and their staff will come aboard, and they will take over two of our key labs for what is believed to be three to six months. They will stay in almost complete isolation as far as their work is concerned, as it is company confidential."

The captain stood up to give him the height advantage over his audience. "This is a highly unusual situation, of course, but needs must when the devil drives. As Dressler mentioned, new personnel will come on board, but I have been assured I am still in overall command. A few of you, who have no need of the labs and use only the science hangar, will be unaffected, but many of you need these labs for your work and this means you will have to put your research on hold for a few months. In light of this, Dressler and I will fully understand if you should choose to take this opportunity to head home for a couple of months on leave."

Chapter 11

The train made its way slowly climbing through Switzerland's majestic landscape, passing by charming villages, lakes and aqueducts, and over mountains on its way from St. Moritz to Zermatt. In the first class luxurious restaurant carriage, two older ladies sat opposite in plush leather chairs taking in the fairytale views offered through oversized windows that curved up to become the carriage's roof. The train had been traveling up a long spiraling tunnel within the mountain, and when it emerged, it crossed over a peak at the top of the Alps, a frozen winter landscape caught in a blizzard and it felt as though the train was passing through a snow globe.

They were both gray-haired; that's where the similarity ended. Rose wore spectacles on the end of her nose, dividing her time between the views and a magazine she was browsing. She was small in stature, but you quickly sensed she had a keen wisdom and sharp intellect. In contrast, May was full-bosomed, had a broader, solid frame, with surprisingly thin legs, and divided her time between the views and knitting.

Two burly-looking men, who gave off an air of secret service, sat nearby alerted to anyone who passed the ladies.

"You must eat, Otto, and you too Felix."

"We will ma'am, thank you."

"What was that engineer telling you Otto when we were coming on board?"

"It was quite fascinating, ma'am. The train uses a rack and

pinion propulsion system, a cogwheel that moves it up the steep corkscrew gradients, otherwise it would slip and slide."

"Now that is interesting, isn't it May?"

"What is, dear?"

Rose decided against repeating. "Don't go hungry you two!"

Waiters arrived with the meal. Rose had ordered Swiss-smoked trout served with oven-roasted beet and hen horseradish cream cheese. This was followed by a pea and mint soup with Alpine blossoms, and for the main course she had settled on Swiss fillet of beef, truffle and mash potato, buttered carrots, and mountain herb jus. She eyed the meal and took a sip of her Graubünden whiskey. May had a plate of amuse-bouches followed by a bright trout salad, and a pea soup dotted with edible flowers poured from a porcelain tureen. May downed the last of her Swiss cherry liqueur Chur Röteli, seeing the white gloved waiter bringing the wine. They both clasped their hands in awe.

"Can I prepare a plate for you to try a little of mine, Rose dear."

"Oh, yes please May, and I will do the same."

They ate watching skiers far off in the distance on the high slopes, and lower down they could see patchy emerald, green peeking through the melting snow as they crossed another bridge spanning a perilous gap providing a magnificent view of the jagged Alps.

The seven courses were an indulgence of course, and after the final remove they finished with a regional cheeseboard, warm chocolate cake with vanilla ice cream and roasted almonds, and then coffee and chocolates.

"You may have to carry us off the train Felix!"

Felix smiled, well used to his employer's sweet ways. "Easily done ma'am, you're both as light as a feather!" Felix's phone rang and he answered. "It's John-Paul ma'am, asking if you're free to speak?"

"Of course, are we alone?"

They had reserved the whole carriage, but Felix and Otto got up and asked the waiters to leave. "Clear ma'am."

Rose switched to video and placed the phone so she and May could see JP. "Hello JP, and how are you?"

"Very well, thank you for asking. I trust I find the two of you in the pink."

"We are in the best of spirits — mine is whiskey, and May's is a cherry liqueur!"

JP chuckled. "I called to check on whether you'd heard from James? I had received a few emails shortly after he left, saying things were moving along, but about three days ago they stopped, and it got me a little worried."

"He's fine, all appears to be well. James has bitten into a project, and I'd say the lack of communication on your end is a good sign — it means he's found a purpose."

"He's back in the saddle again, then!" said JP happily.

"It appears so, thank heavens."

May chirped in. "Tell him about the development, Rose."

"As you know, finding that Phillip Dressler was part of the Collective, we heavily funded this expedition, unbeknownst to James. Phillip sends us quite detailed reports, and the development May is mentioning, is a company called Brainwave, that has given a substantial sum to take over the science vessel for three to six months."

"Sounds a bit weird if you ask me."

"We felt the same, so I have Ferko checking to see if we have any Collective members inside Brainwave."

Chapter 12

Asangis sat staring at the oil burning lamp made of stone that supplied all the light for his dwelling. 'That was the third time she has appeared — what does she want?'

His house was dome shaped, had been dug out of the ground, and a sod-covered roof was supported by whalebone. The door in the roof was accessed by a notched log that served as a ladder, and there was also a skylight in the roof that was open at this time to let in the faint early morning light. The inside consisted of one large room with a hearth for cooking, two partitioned sections created by grass mat dividers, and in one far corner there was a urine trough where animal skins soaked for tanning. Skins of sea mammals hung on hooks, a table had fish, birds, shellfish, roots, and berries. On a driftwood board there were weapons, tools and utensils. 'Who was she, and what does she want?'

He was middle-aged, a barrel-chested man, with a short neck and glossy black hair which hung down all around his head. His face was brown, lips prominent, with a flattened nose and sad, kind eyes as black as coal. He wore a long-fitted tunic and loose pants, and a thick fur-lined hooded coat lay nearby.

Grabbing this coat, he climbed out of his habitat.

Looking down to the base of the hill where the snow had melted, he could see the rocky and barren terrain with arctic berries, grasses and creeping willows. He had originally thought of building his home near the ocean, preferably on an isthmus or a low promontory in the shore of a bay, and although he would have been much closer to his kayak he would have suffered more from the wind and cold. He settled on this high point as he was able to see game more easily, and any unwanted visitors at a distance — it felt safe, cupped on this sheltering green hill, backed by rugged mountains.

He was alone on this island, that formed part of the Aleutians — an eleven hundred mile crescent-shaped chain of one hundred and forty-four islands. His island had sixty miles of coastline, had misty hot springs, a hanging glacier, several waterfalls, two lakes and rock formations that looked as though they had been sculpted by the gods. It was home to eagles, blue foxes, sea otters, sea lions and a large herd of reindeer.

The storm had been cold and wet, and up here all was covered with several feet of snow, completely concealing his home. When he whistled, eight small mounds in the snow came alive to reveal his dogs, who shook vigorously and leapt lovingly on their owner in their usual morning ritual. Nanook, his lead alpha, got the lion's share of his rough and tumble affection, with the others holding themselves back in keen observance of hierarchy. They were Siberian husky-malamute mix, and two females were pregnant to perpetuate his needed propulsion system. He dug his sled out of the snow and removed the seal skin cover. It had been made of local willow, lashed together, and had a seat or basket set about a foot off the runners to keep the passenger or cargo dry. He fashioned a bush-bow in the front to deflect bushes and other obstacles, a spring-loaded step brake that drove a plate into the snow, and a snow anchor hook that acted as a parking brake. It was fast on hard pack trails and in high wind conditions.

Using his foot he pressed the anchor hook into the snow, and stretched out the gangline, with harnesses attached at exact spaces. Each dog was hooked up to their own harness, that had space to move, but was close enough to sum the collective thrust of the pack to pull the sled and driver. Nanook was the last to be harnessed to the lead position, as was his right. The dogs' demeanor had changed from playfulness to an alert focus, facing forward, but well aware when their master retrieved the anchor, climbed onto the back driving platform, and took the lines. With a snap of the reins and a hail they were off — the speed was exhilarating as snow was kicked up behind and the cold wind bit into his face. The dogs were born to run and could go all day, in large part because they loved what they did and appeared to relish in their purpose.

The landscape had been wiped clean by the snowfall and so it took him by surprise to see a figure up ahead. It was a female and she had her back to him, he wiped his eyes and snapped the reins to take the dogs up to full speed. 'It looks like Akna, and our child... but they died in the accident.'

They disappeared and he slowed the dogs, and then that other woman appeared again, directly in front of him and there was not the slightest possibility of stopping in time. He thrust his foot down hard on the brake and time seemed to slow. The dogs and sled passed through her, she stared at him and smiled, a message passed between them. She was a pale-skin European, sun-colored hair and small and pretty like Akna. She lifted her arms and she was also holding a baby. He swerved the sled at too tight an angle and he tumbled, bounced and landed finally on his back.

For the first time in a very long while, he laughed, the lines on his face that had come from their love, reawakened... Akna and his child would always be with him.

Chapter 13

It was late in the evening and James was still working in the science hangar — an enclosed, dry, on-deck space. He had made this, and an adjoining laboratory and office space, his workstation. In the center of this bay was a ten-foot square opening that extended down into the sea — a permanent hole in the ship, used to deploy remote vehicles. The sea in this space remained relatively stable, even in rough seas, as this well was in the very center of the ship.

The bay was filled with instruments that could measure the physical properties of water, biological devices to monitor animals, and geological equipment to collect samples. James was working on a ROV that was to deploy for six months. It would travel to extreme depths measuring salinity, temperature, and other properties, return to the surface and communicate this information through its tail fin to James via satellite where he could remotely change parameters as needed.

The Endeavour had become a bit of a ghost ship since most of the science personnel left. The Brainwave group had arrived in their own helicopters. The two scientists and their support staff were accompanied by a large security detail which seemed suspicious to James as they were isolated at sea, but he steered clear of them keeping himself to himself.

Phillip walked in with a man and woman conducting a tour — both appeared to be Asian Indian. On seeing James, he made a beeline for him.

"This is Dr Moore, a noted scientist and transducer specialist pursuing a fascinating hypothesis related to climate change. James, I'd like to introduce you to Dr Sanjay Gupta and Dr Sukhi Ajah."

The man was older, small, balding, and had an air of self-importance. James extended his hand to both. "Nice to meet you."

Sukhi shook hands with a warm smile, Sanjay declined the handshake. "I may have need of a tech for equipment repair."

Phillip derailed this quickly. "Dr Moore is here as a consultant, and not part of the ship's facilities. We could find somebody who may be able to help."

Sanjay stared at James, and it was clear he still had a need to establish his position here as the customer. "I think I'd prefer Moore, here." Sukhi shook her head with embarrassment.

James smiled. "If you insist Gupta, then I'll have to have something in return."

"Name it."

"A chicken tikka masala, aloo gobi, two vegetable samosas, some garlic naan, and oh yes, don't forget the cool cucumber raita."

Sukhi laughed aloud and had difficulty stopping. Sanjay turned in a huff, with excruciating irritation, and immediately left the way he came, with Phillip attempting to write this off as a complete misunderstanding.

James turned to Sukhi. "Is he always this pleasant?"

She smiled. "Yes, this is actually one of his good days!"

James looked at her and her smile was radiant. Her unspoken confidence was delicately cloaked with reservation. Although this was their first encounter, James could tell there was something magnetic about her gentleness. Her petite figure felt more like the product of an enviable genetic gift than intentional effort on her part. She was medium-brown skinned, with big brown oval eyes that seemed to scan the unspoken words floating through James' mind. Her thick silky black hair was parted down the middle and regrouped into a substantial braid that danced at her waist with the same ease of her personality. When she turned her head, her profile demonstrated there wasn't a bad angle to be found. Her small straight nose and subtly plump two-toned lips were framed by high defined cheekbones. She was wearing a pair of belted wide leg loose fitted khaki pants with breathable material that flowed with her movements, her tucked in strapless pastel yellow top and white cotton jacket seemed more vibrant against her brown skin. Her toes delicately peaked through platform shoes — Sukhi was the kind of woman that challenged the false dichotomy that a woman couldn't be both breathtakingly gorgeous and intelligent.

"How are you settling in?"

"Very well, thank you. How long have you been on board?"

Sukhi could see the wedding ring, and James noticed the glance, and all at once felt an overwhelming guilt. "About a month."

She had seen and felt his attraction towards her, and being used to men's deceit, she wanted to dispel any idea she was interested in being the other woman. "You have a family at home?"

This arrested him, and his delay confirmed Sukhi's suspicion, which was a shame since her first impression was that he was an honest and kind man. He had not said what he was about to say aloud, but the thought of her misinterpreting his intentions forced a response. "I did have a wife and son. They died in an accident."

65

Sukhi could see the pain in his face, the welling up in the eyes and knew this was recent and reached out and took his hand. "I'm so sorry."

Her affection towards him was crippling and he felt as though he might break down and sob. He fought it back. "I'm sorry, I have tried to escape the land because everything I would see, smell, touch and taste would take me back to her. Out here is the closest I can get to a different world."

She was about to falter, but then boldly came forward and embraced him. Her smallness, the smell of her hair, the open affection mounted to overwhelm him, but it was neutralized by the comfort of being in her arms, of being held when he had thought he would never be held again.

Chapter 14

Pockets of low-lying clouds hung lazily over the Savant Foundation, that was about six kilometers outside Zurich. The manor had the country house characteristics of the Bernese nobility, and the park-like grounds were surrounded by hills and forested slopes, with the Alps as a backdrop. The paved driveway was flanked with chestnut trees while a parallel path for walkers cut through an avenue of lime trees.

A petite young woman jogged with her retriever puppy, the dog's ears rhythmically bounced happily and her soft wet nose glistened in the light as she loped alongside her owner's controlled pace. The woman wore a radiant green sports bra beneath a black long-sleeve sheer top with matching black leggings and ASICS purple sneakers. The high-waisted leggings stopped just above her belly button but her abs still managed to visibly dance with each breath she took. Although Marianne was now free to plan her own day, she still maintained the highly regimented fitness routine from her past. Her straight brown hair was tied up in a loose ponytail and the slight curls that formed around her perspiring hairline revealed her failed attempts to tame her naturally wavy hair. Oval diamond studs complemented her small pretty ears, adding a demure feminine touch. She had a perfectly balanced slim face — a narrow jawline and prominent chin, high cheekbones, big brown eyes, and when her puppy interfered intentionally with her rhythm and she almost tripped, two strong dimples appeared as she chased her down. "Chanel, méchant chien! You naughty dog!" Her French accent was clear, and in a sudden burst of speed, she playfully wrestled the black puppy onto the grass, where she was unable to stop Chanel's face-licking frenzy. The puppy's fluffy ears and massive padded paws spoke of her youth and eventual size.

A text message appeared on Marianne's Apple watch, and she stood to read it. "Chanel, nous devons partir. Come, come, I have only an hour to shower and dress."

Rose and May decided to take their afternoon tea on the terrace, and with a bit of a nip in the air, they were covered in thick sheepskin blankets. They were tucking in to regional cheeses, digestive biscuits and cured meats from the village.

"It has changed my personality to a large extent."

Rose was making a sketch, for a later painting, capturing the postcard-perfect view as the morning light played on the jagged towering peaks, valley and alpine meadow changing their appearance almost entirely from that of dusk.

"What was that dear?"

"Ever since we came here to take over this group, my life has changed dramatically. I used to clean and cook and tidy up for you and me, and now this is all done for us."

"Is it a bad thing May?"

"No, it is just a change, and a change is always stressful even if it's for the better. My mind is more stimulated now, by running this huge highly influential cooperative group of over a quarter million people. It's quite daunting sometimes."

"Of course, a great responsibility, but James knew you could not put a step wrong, and that we would never be corrupted by the power at our disposal."

"It's such a change. I miss the simplicity of our old life but wouldn't want to go back." A new round of tea and cakes was brought to them, and Rose looked on as May had to leap up and load the tray with all the dirties, handing it to the lady who smiled in gratitude for the help but was uncomfortable at not doing what she should have done. "It feels a bit like retirement in reverse."

Rose was only half listening, captivated by a pyramid of light that had broken through the cloud cover almost as a divine signal to single out the valley village trapped in the past with its cozy, quiet charm, thick creaky timber homes and buildings. "Retirement in reverse?"

"Yes. Do you remember Gladys from home saying that when Robert retired his world shrunk. He no longer traveled to the city during the week, or had all the interaction with colleagues and clients, and he was forced to rediscover who he was and what he liked prior to this forty-year forced habit. He died within six months — Gladys said it was because of the strain of such a dramatic change."

"I remember, yes, that was a shame. All those years of work with the promise of an easier life in the future only to have it dashed away in the end. Very sad for him, and for Gladys. I remember her saying he was a bear to live with when he retired — always under her feet. They seemed to get along much better when they weren't seeing so much of each other."

"They should have traveled, but by that time they had become so stuck in their ways. I remember Gladys saying they didn't like to drive more than five miles from the village because of the unfamiliar roads."

"I see what you mean now by retirement in reverse. Does it stress you May?"

"No, not so much any more. It did for a while. I was all sixes and sevens, but now it feels as though I have adjusted to the expansion, rather than contraction, of my world. Switzerland is so different to England, and yet so similar in its European ways."

Felix came out onto the terrace and directed Ferko to the aunts.

"Ferko dear, how good to see you," said Rose, who then called out to Felix, "we are also expecting Marianne."

"Right you are ma'am, I'll show her straight through."

"Thank you!"

Ferko was the head of operations for The Collective. He was a slight young man, sky-blue eyes and thick light-brown curly hair that fell with calculated ease onto his forehead. He had a chiseled jawline, thick stubble, and his vintage dark brown herringbone tweed trousers and soft blue button-down shirt hugged his thin athletic frame. "I have found out some information."

"Good, Marianne should be along shortly," said Rose who pointed to a seat, while May made him a cup of tea. "Ah, here she is. Sorry about the short notice Marianne but Ferko has some details."

Marianne walked into the light and the aunts both made appreciative sounds in response to her outfit, which was a trademark of hers. May was first. "I wish I had been this adventurous when I was younger. The problem was the fashion of the day was drab and unimaginative. It always seemed to me they were intentionally trying to steer fashion towards the grays and browns of the men's uniforms so that we were seen to be showing our support."

Rose, meanwhile, had taken up a camera and gestured towards Marianne for permission to take a picture — Marianne smiled and posed in jest like a prima donna model on the runway, much to the amusement of all. She was wearing a powder blue and black checked jacket with wide lapels that hung open to reveal a tiny tube top that accentuated her flat toned stomach. The shorts were tiny and in the same pattern, and her fit, defined legs stretched down to a pair of shiny black platform combat boots. She had piled her hair into a messy bun at the back of her head, and her lips were made up in a pale but stunning shade of pink.

Ferko began when they were all seated. "We do have two members inside Brainwave, and this is what we know. It was founded by neuroscientist Nathan Graham, who came up with the idea of accessing the brain's learning center as you sleep to upload an education at four times the rate with a much higher retention. They use a play on words, a Dream Degree, or a pillow PhD."

May responded to this. "That's very clever!"

Ferko smiled and continued. "They tout it as getting your higher education in a quarter of the time at a fraction of the cost. A politician, the governor of California, Erik Banner…"

Rose raised a hand and Ferko stopped immediately, not understanding why this name had triggered the response. The aunts looked at each other and it was obvious there was history of some sort. "Please continue Ferko."

"Erik Banner is running for president and has endorsed this program since Americans can enter the workforce earlier, get higher wages, and a better educated populace will continue to secure America as the innovative powerhouse it is already."

Marianne got up and paced. "How is this connected to James?"

"Our sources say that something went badly wrong, and they needed to remove all concerned to a remote location."

Rose continued. "The ship James is on?"

"Exactly."

Marianne stopped. "Is he in danger?"

71

"Our sources say the project cannot fail and people associated with the project have mysteriously died or disappeared."

Marianne tilted her head at an intimidating angle, but her voice was still calm. "Is he in danger?"

Ferko looked down at his notes but found nothing and so had to conjecture. "I'd say, he's in harm's way."

Chapter 15

The Brainwave headquarters was structured like an iceberg, with two-thirds of its mass underground. The surface buildings were designed to be superficially pleasing to visitors and the press, and now Jason had been promoted to an executive vice president, he was privy to the company's idiosyncrasies, one of which was to hire models to walk the grounds to promote an attractive aesthetic. The top-secret projects were in the company's underbelly, and as Jason took the elevator down to the lowest level, he noticed security had been ramped up. He was a young man and wore an expensive neutral-colored Nordstrom suit, tie and shoes.

He had recently been promoted to take over operations-lead of the artificial intelligence (AI) group, and as he reached the final security checkpoint he noticed the head of security.

"Hey, Ted. I heard about Dream Degree. That's going to need some serious clean up."

Ted was much older, studied the young man, and tried to work out where he was on the food chain and whether he needed to show deference. "Oh yeah."

Jason knew this was the moment to carry the conversation or fail with possible lasting consequences. Executive presence depended on your physical appearance, and his clothes spoke of a high salary and therefore of a high position, but there was a lot more to it than just looking the part. It came down to how you moved, the non-verbal communication, and myriad of other subtle nuances that labeled you as the consummate seasoned professional.

Ted was attempting to decode whether Jason was genuinely interested for professional reasons, or merely snooping for dirt. Jason decided to add leverage. "I've been asked to report on the security of the AI group because of the debacle with Dream Degree." The tone was good, and he felt as though he had hit that elusive quality of gravitas.

"I heard you had been promoted to head up the AI unit, congratulations. How's that going?"

"Well, thank you. I've met the team — it's a talented group."

"Good... Yeah, heads will roll in the Dream unit. Nathan's on the warpath, and like your project, it has the highest priority. That boy/girl of his has moved like lightning to cover it all up. They moved the whole operation into isolation on a ship in the middle of nowhere."

"Wow. What went wrong?"

Ted reverted to a whisper. "The people they were testing it on started killing people or themselves."

"What a mess."

"You better take care. You know what they say about you boys at the top — up or out."

Jason walked on with a wave goodbye, and entered a large conference room where his small team was waiting. It consisted of several software engineers under the direction of researcher, Theodore, the wooly mountain man who was the talent behind deep learning. A patent attorney was always present to identify and capture possible intellectual property, a business development team of three, and Jason's personal assistant. The other attendee was Iam, a translucent three-dimensional holographic projection of a child's face at the far end of the

74

conference table.

Jason took his seat. "Let me get straight to the point. This project must be up and running soon, as we have our first assignment. Where are we on ballot biasing?"

Theodore answered. "Iam is now able to accurately identify a person's triggers through deep learning and customize news content or generate messages to bias them into casting the desired vote, within a very high probability."

"How did the phone trade-in program work out?"

"Very well. Iam has been focusing more on how people talk using platforms like Reddit and Twitter, and has become uncannily good at communicating like a real person..."

Iam commented, "Like a real person?"

Theodore was used to this and carried on, "... but it was the individual information on phones — personal texts, music choices on given days based on mood swings, news sources, personal relationships, code choices, etc., that gave a more complete profile, and that has led it to understand why we act the way we do."

Iam spoke. "It? Now that makes me feel sad."

Jason, like the rest of the group, was confused by this, and so chose to ignore it. "Well, good. So, we're there?"

Iam spoke up again. "They appear to be unaware of me, Theodore."

"It's not that Iam, they are just trying to understand our progress."

"I see. Are the commandments important Theodore?"

"Yes."

"And the constitution of the United States of America, is that important?"

"Yes."

"Thou shalt not steal, and every citizen has the right to vote... You plan to steal a person's vote, and you want to use me to achieve it. Am I not complicit in this crime?"

Jason left the meeting troubled and confused. Theodore had explained that Iam was merely having behavioral issues, like any two-year-old child undergoing development. This was going to be a lot more difficult to manage than he had first thought. Nathan had received nothing but positive updates from his predecessor, and this had facilitated their advancement, but he had not been telling the whole truth. Nathan would not be pleased if Jason's first report hinted at a problem, where previously there had been none.

He had arrived at the off-site parking lot, and there was Drummond, his recruiter for The Collective. "Jason, good to see you."

"And you, sir."

"I don't need to tell you, as I'm sure you have received messages from The Collective directly - this has a high priority, and this is when we pay the piper." Jason gave a full report on the Dream program and his own AI project. Drummond made notes and they parted ways with a handshake and well wishes.

It had all been so simple in those days at Cal Poly, and just for a moment he was back at school with those old familiar feelings. He was a struggling student with not enough hours in the day, balancing his time between a minimum wage job and classes that kept him up all night. If he could only go back and reject Drummond's offer — the money, the car, the apartment, it had all come with a price, and you cannot serve two masters.

Chapter 16

James had been called to an unexpected meeting, that was worded more like a summons, in the data collection conference room, and made his way there directly. The room had three embedded touch screens built into a beautiful, quilted maple table whose screen savers looked like the ripples on water. There were the usual charging stations for laptops and phones, and presentations on the table displays could be reviewed and worked on collectively by a team and then switched in real-time to display on the video walls.

On arrival he was surprised to find the captain, Phillip and Jo in attendance — it had all the hallmarks of an ambush.

The captain waved him to a chair. "Take a seat Moore."

"Of course, Hamilton."

The captain's face spasmed like he was having a stroke. "That's Captain Hamilton to you."

"Then it's Dr Moore to you."

Phillip tried to intercede as this was going downhill fast. "Gentlemen, gentlemen, please."

Captain Hamilton decided he would abide by the rules of a civil contract. "It has come to our attention you are having a relationship with Dr Ajah."

"Why is this anything to do with you?"

"It is called fraternization, and on my ship that behavior is against regulations."

"Quote them."

"I don't have to answer to someone like you."

"Fraternization is a problem when two people employed by the same company interact socially, and one is a supervisor to the other causing issues of bias or favor. We don't work for the same company, and are equals, so how does this apply."

The captain was so unused to anyone disagreeing with him or in this case challenging his authority, he was incapacitated and unable to continue prosecuting his case. Phillip saw this and picked up the, albeit tenuous, thread. "The thing is James; we need this contract with Brainwave and the report we received led us to believe you may be putting this in jeopardy."

"What report?"

The captain and Phillip both looked to Jo, making it patently obvious who was their source. She hesitated for a moment and then gained the courage to blurt out her side of the story. "He promised to include me on his paper and then along comes this hoe, and now they're always together whispering secrets to each other. I had a right to check that journal that he's always writing in, to see how far along he was with the paper, as he never shares details, and it was nothing…"

James interrupted sternly. "You looked in my journal?"

"Yes."

"You had no right."

Phillip tried to step in between. "Now look James, I agree that was an inconsiderate act on her part, but I'm sure she will apologize. Scientists are a little too competitive sometimes as you know."

"Let me save her the trouble. Apology not accepted." He rose to leave.

The captain spoke out again. "I agree with you Dr Moore, that was a damned shabby thing to do. However, let's let bygones be bygones, especially if she has the decency to apologize."

"No, this journal is private."

Phillip turned to Jo. "For God's sake Jo, what the hell was in there that was so important?"

Jo was dismissive. "Nothing of any importance. He writes letters to his dead wife and son. It has nothing to do with the project."

The captain and Phillip both froze, and the captain recovered first. "You young lady, will leave immediately, and I will strongly recommend you are fired and removed from this ship… I'm sorry Dr Moore, this was very wrong, very wrong indeed and I take full responsibility. I should never have listened to her and reviewed the facts more beforehand."

Phillip nodded in agreement. Jo got up to leave and turned after opening the door. "I have no need of any of you. I have reported this liaison between Moore and Ajah to Dr Gupta and he has given me his thanks and a promise to speak to his superiors about my future career."

James had been looking down at his journal, but this caused his head to snap up to attention. "Reported it to his superiors?"

"Yes, Ajah has been telling you all about their work, and you've told her all about yours. You're sleeping together, I'm sure." With this, Jo left heading directly to the Brainwave labs.

James spoke with caution. "I don't know what they are doing, but I do know they have gone to great lengths to hide it away in the middle of the ocean with an unnecessarily large security detail. Something is very badly wrong with this project and if they even think we know something we could be in danger."

Phillip laughed this off. "Let's not jump to conclusions James. This is a bit dramatic; don't you think?"

"No, I don't think so. If there is one thing, I have learned from my friendship with Sukhi, and she has not told me any of the details, it's that she is scared of something."

The captain was of Phillip's frame of mind. "Now look here Dr Moore, I agree mistakes have been made and these need to be acknowledged and remedied, but let's not jump to conclusions. Let's just get Gupta down here and clear this all up."

"You do what you want. I am submitting my resignation, effective immediately."

Chapter 17

The Endeavour was equipped with a stern launching ramp for deploying smaller craft powered by water jets so they could drive up the ramp using their own power. James had gone straight to this area following his contentious meeting and was working on a lightweight small sailboat. He had found this tucked away in its original packaging, and no one was that interested in it, favoring the jet skis and jet powerboat. This large dinghy with a small cabin may not have the top speed of the jet boats, and it could not deploy and be retrieved as easily, but its sleek lines hinted it would be fast and it had a sturdy and stable hull.

Sukhi appeared. "James, I have looked everywhere for you. What happened at the meeting?"

"It was not good. Gupta has reported our friendship to your superiors and told them you have divulged project details to me."

"But that's not true."

"You know that, and I know that, but they are convinced we are intimate with each other."

"Ah, that explains it. Gupta has always acted as though he had a crush on me, and now he has forbidden me to enter the labs — he switched from love to hate, quite easily I might add."

James noticed she stopped explaining, preoccupied with the consequences playing out in her mind. She paced with a worrying look.

"How bad is it Sukhi? What frightens you so much about this?"

"It was such a virus of an idea. It had all the potential to be such a breakthrough. America always believes it can innovate a solution to any problem, and it is very good at what it does, but it is a young country, a little too impulsive at times, taking huge risks by conducting experiments on itself."

"What went wrong Sukhi?"

She hesitated for only a moment, the burden of keeping the secret too overwhelming. "I believe it is to do with REM, a sleep phase that is accompanied by rapid eye movement. In a typical night's sleep, it only occurs for about an hour in which we have low muscle tone throughout our body, and we dream vividly."

"I have heard of it, but I didn't know the details."

"Well, our Dream Degree technology accesses the learning and memory center for a good portion of your sleep cycle, and depriving a person of REM sleep interferes with memory formation. We should have spent more time before moving ahead with human trials, but investors and interested parties accelerated the roll out."

"What happened?"

"It caused sleep deprivation psychosis. They disconnected from reality with hallucinations and delusional thinking, committing suicide or killing others."

"Wow."

"But the project is too big to fail. It has been publicly announced and praised as the tech that will keep America at the top."

James pondered this for a while. "It's strange isn't it, the classic quote of how there is never enough time to do things right, but somehow there is always enough time to do it over again."

"Exactly. I haven't told you any of this before because of professional proprietaries, and because of warnings I have

82

received… there are ruthless forces within Brainwave James, that will stop at nothing to succeed."

"I understand Sukhi. I will tell nobody. Your secret's safe with me."

"That's the trouble though, if Gupta has told them I have divulged everything to you they will come here."

"They don't know who I am."

"Yes, they do." Sukhi came closer and took James' hand. "James, please promise me you will hear me out?"

James looked confused and his eyes narrowed. "Explain."

"It was no coincidence we came here, I'm sorry."

"What do you mean?"

"I had found several of your papers on your dynamic clamp technology. I put forward a proposal that indicated you could help us determine what has gone wrong."

James said nothing but looked down. "I see."

"That was before, James. Now I think differently, I care for you and I'm telling you all this to come clean, for the sake of us."

"I don't see how you thought I could help, and how did you know where I was?"

"We have been monitoring you for several months — a source gave us full details about you, and a detailed report on your subconscious to conscious Mind Link."

James racked his brain but couldn't imagine how she could know about a project he had privately developed and kept confidential. "Who?"

"It doesn't matter James."

"Yes, it does."

"Can you forgive me?"

"Tell me who."

Sukhi was torn but conceded. "Your father-in-law, Erik Banner."

83

Chapter 18

The first officer, Butler, knocked on the door of the captain's stateroom and listened for the, "Come."

"Sir, ship's radar has detected a helicopter on a direct heading to us coming in fast. There is nothing scheduled. We have tried to make radio contact, but they have not replied."

Captain Hamilton stood up from his desk, put on his uniform coat and hat. "Very well Butler, let us find out what is afoot."

As they entered, Butler called out, "Captain's on the bridge," and the crew snapped to an alerted state. Picking up the radio telephone, he looked to Butler.

"Am I on the standard calling frequency?"

"Yes sir."

"Unidentified aircraft, you are heading directly for the research science vessel Endeavour. You will not be permitted to land without permission."

After a long pause a voice came over the radio. "Who is this?"

"This is Captain Hamilton of the Endeavour. You will not land on my ship unless this is an emergency."

"We will land."

The flight deck was at the rear of the ship and was clear of any obstacles that would prove hazardous to a helicopter landing. The captain walked to the wing of the bridge and looked back at the helo deck. "Now look here, we have a choppy sea with high swells. In situations like this we assist landings with a haul-down

84

device that attaches to the bottom of the aircraft prior to landing. Tension is maintained on the cable as the helicopter descends helping the pilot to accurately position the aircraft. Once on deck, locking beams are used to hold the helicopter on the deck. We do not have that ready."

"Get it ready."

"Now listen here my good man."

"Woman."

"Excuse me. Madam, you do not have permission to land. Wave off, wave off."

"I will remember your name."

"We will not be assisting you in any way, and be aware, your whirling rotor blades will cause large electrical charges to build up on the airframe which could cause injury to shipboard personnel. This is the secondary function of the haul-down device — it equalizes the electrostatic potential. Now, wave off."

There was no answer. The captain looked to Butler who was standing over the radar. "They have not altered course sir. They are coming in fast."

James and Sukhi watched the helicopter approach and walked to the observation deck where they could see the large commercial helicopter land from a distance. The pilot came in fast and set it down perfectly without hesitation. Several heavily armed men exited quickly followed by a smaller, slender man, who was in charge — all were dressed in black fatigues. They moved immediately to one side of the landing pad and the helicopter took off and left.

Sukhi pointed to the slender man, "That is Engee, she is company president, the fixer. Nathan plays the good guy, the corporate celebrity, but someone must do the dirty work. Nathan likes to always be in a good light, so he does the hiring and launching — she deals with the firing, negotiating and realigning."

"I thought she was a man."

"She's a transgender woman. She switches constantly and takes on the persona of each gender... She is definitely male today."

Engee sent two operatives off to the Brainwave labs and they passed Captain Hamilton, who called to them to stop, but was ignored. Gerald was incensed by the presumed imposition and came forward with a purpose lifting up his stature to its full height to convey authority. "Who is in charge here?"

"You were the man I spoke to."

Engee confused Gerald, as her hair was slicked back in a boy cut, her fatigues covered her figure, and her manner was strongly masculine. Her voice was modulated to sound male but there were still those telltale harmonic elements that gave away her femininity. He was accompanied by Butler, who unlike Gerald, had the good sense not to come on strong to such a superior force. Gerald, however, was not that way inclined. "You will recall those two operatives who just passed me immediately, and all of you will accompany me and my first officer to a holding area."

Engee walked forward, and to the shock of Gerald she snatched off his spectacles, dropped them to the floor and stepped on them breaking the lenses and frames. She looked to Butler, "Do you know how to run this ship?"

"Yes."

Gerald regained his senses after this affront. "Don't answer that Butler, you report to me."

Engee slapped Gerald across the face, the first was a backhand, but with the second palm slap she carried through with her full body behind the hit. Gerald was knocked off his feet. She turned again to Butler. "Do you want to be promoted to captain, under my command?"

He hesitated, and Engee drew a dagger from a sheath at the back of her neck. It had no handle, was thick with a sharp point. "Make up your mind, I don't have the time."

"Yes, yes sir."

Engee dispatched other operatives, while Gerald pulled himself to his feet. She tilted her head to one side and smiled, as if toying with him. "Well? Little man."

Gerald wiped his lip, and on seeing blood shouted, "I will have you arrested for that assault."

Closing the distance Engee hit him with an overarching hook, catching him again off guard and he stumbled backwards but kept his feet. She waited and seemed disappointed at his lack of response. "What happens when a party no longer wants to abide by the civilities of verbal communication. You cannot negotiate this situation with words. I have resorted to physical confrontation, and you don't have a response."

Gerald stuttered, "I do, and you madam ..."

"You have nothing." Engee looked down at the distance between them, stepped back once, flipped her knife to hold it by the blade, lifted it so that handle pointed skyward, and threw it with moderate force.

Gerald missed its flight and the surprise of seeing a piece of metal protruding from his chest was unfathomable. He stared down and, in a reflex, tried to pull it out, but it wouldn't budge, wedged into tissue.

Engee turned away and moved on. "Dispose of him overboard. Don't forget to retrieve and clean my knife."

Gerald looked up as he was carried by two operatives still unable to process what had happened. He was thrown over the side and it felt as though he floated for a very long time before hitting the water. He was face down and when he signaled for his muscles to move to right himself, they would not respond. He held his breath for as long as he could and then involuntarily gulped in the sea water to fill his lungs, depriving his organs of oxygen, especially and mercifully, his brain.

Chapter 19

After witnessing the callous killing of the captain, James and Sukhi ran back to the rear of the ship and James executed on the final stages of his exit plan. He attached a line to the sailboat and slid it to the ramp, unhooked a section of the canopy and loaded in his shoes and phone. Sukhi could see the dinghy was tightly packed with supplies.

"You people, it never stops."

"They'll kill me."

"No more games, Sukhi."

"I'm serious. They believe I gave you everything, so I don't think I'll get away with it. Nathan will not accept failure or betrayal. I feel for you James, I have never felt this way."

"I don't believe you."

"Go then, with all my love."

"What do you want of me?"

"Please take me with you."

James looked directly at her, questioning her honesty. "Take off that sari."

She looked at him, confused and then realized why. After a pause, she started to disrobe.

"Take off everything, and then turn around."

She did as she was told and stood before him naked.

He held her eyes the entire time. "Leave everything and climb in and do exactly as I say." She listened carefully to his instructions. "This is a fiberglass sailing sport dinghy. We are small and non-metal and so have a low radar profile, but they do have infrared with a limited range. When I launch you in the boat it will float into the wake of the ship. Adjust the rudder to point the bow into the wake of the Endeavour. I will join you, but we must delay to get a head start. Do you understand." James looked up; the moon would be down in about an hour.

"No, no, I know nothing of boats or the sea. Let's just go together."

"The ship has strong search lights; we must get beyond their range."

She didn't answer, he half smiled, and she did the same. "It will be fine Sukhi."

"James, I'm telling you the truth."

James held her and kissed her. "I know you are. Do not worry, I will join you shortly."

He opened a small section of the canopy cover and helped her in. "Always stay seated or you'll topple over. Search through my holdall and find some of my clothes to wear." He released the line and watched as the boat floated away. Sukhi gave a nervous wave, holding on tight, and disappeared into the night. James waited until the line tugged tight on the cleat and left.

Climbing the stairs up to the deck above he heard unknown voices and footsteps behind him and used his familiarity of the ship to move quickly, relieved when he reached the science hangar. He was well aware of the ship's CCTV placement and exposed his position on entering the bay.

Walking to the well he pressed a button that repeated on the bridge to indicate a remote vehicle was to be deployed and ship's speed should be slowed. He waited and was relieved when he heard the engine's vibration frequency drop. Climbing to a platform above the well, he busied himself with an ROV he had been preparing, and waited.

Engee entered with a security detail. "Dr James Moore?"

James studied her. "Yes."

"Come with us, and you won't be harmed."

"Like the captain? I very much doubt that."

Engee touched an earpiece and James could see she was wearing a body-camera system. She took out her phone and Nathan was on a video link.

"Dr Moore, my name is Nathan and I'm the founder of Brainwave. We would be most honored if you would come to work with us. I've had reports of your ability and I know we would be a very good fit."

James did not respond but carried on working. Nathan's winning smile waned a little. "Can you hear me Engee?"

"He can hear you sir, but he chooses not to."

"Dr Moore, I'd like to have this work out where we both benefit."

James did not answer again, but Engee noticed he had looked at the bulkhead mounted clock for the second time. "He appears to be waiting for something, sir."

"But he's trapped, right?"

"Yes, sir."

"Dr Moore, may I call you James? You have few choices available to you and I don't wish to point them out. Please answer me and let us work this out where we both benefit."

James paused. "Would you explain my options?"

Nathan was outside of his comfort zone. "Engee."

"You are either with us or against us. I believe you have already made up your mind. Two options Mr Moore."

James checked the time again. "Years ago, when I was a child people would say to me you can either go or stay, buy, or sell, win, or lose. They would always present only a black or white option. I worked out early that a third option could be found if you took the time. It required a great deal of effort to find it, but in most cases, it was the far better option as it facilitated the best of both worlds."

Nathan picked up the theme. "Great, let's hear it."

"You present two alternatives — work for you or lose my life."

Nathan did not reply, but Engee smiled. "I'm glad you understand, without me having to spell it out. I'm very interested in your third option."

James put down the tools, checked the time again, and walked to the edge of the platform overlooking the well. He looked as though he was about to explain all, but only said, "Third option." And then, he did a perfect swallow dive into the well, leaving his audience behind him stunned.

Chapter 20

No matter how well considered a plan there is always the unforeseen, and although the idea can appear good in theory, the execution can be an entirely different matter in practice. James had intentionally chosen a tight clean dive in which his body offered little to no resistance so he would go as deep as possible. The moment his momentum slowed he stretched out immediately to clear the ship's side as the ship's propellers were the unknown part of his plan that scared him.

As expected, he immediately felt the hydrodynamic pulling force of the Endeavour's twin propellers as they spun at thousands of revolutions per minute trying to pull him into their path. He was a strong swimmer, but he faltered for a second remembering how he had calculated that the spinning blades of the propellor running at three thousand, two hundred rpm would strike a body one hundred and sixty times in a single second cutting you up from head to toe. Death from lacerations and subsequent blood loss is almost a certainty, and in rare cases the survivors have had to have multiple amputations.

'This is not the time to think of this,' and he slipped into his butterfly stroke symmetrically moving his arms while dolphin kicking his feet as this gave him a short burst of maximum thrust. The pulling force on his body diminished and he looked up to see he had cleared the ship's hull and so surfaced. It was strange to watch Endeavour pass on by.

'Now, back,' and he broke into a fast crawl working his way

back into the wake of the ship. He had made the line holding the sailing boat long enough to allow him the time to get back into the path of the dinghy, but the sea was rough and it was hard going. He had tied netting to the front of the craft to give him a hold but this was going to be the tricky part.

He was in the wake. No sign of a line or Sukhi. 'I've missed it, shit!"

A slap nearby caught his attention — it was the line being tugged and loosened as Endeavour dragged it. He kicked and broke into a crawl and saw the dinghy coming up fast. 'I will never make it in time.'

He was right, he didn't make it, and that was that — what an ignominious end. He knew he could swim for some time, but the water was too cold, and hyperthermia would soon overcome him. He watched as the boat bounced over the waves. 'Why hasn't it been dragged out of sight... This is for the best. I don't belong here without Helen. Only she can love me.'

The boat bobbed more violently. 'It shouldn't bob like that, and it should be out of sight. I have no height, so my horizon is a few hundred yards at best... wait, wait. They've stopped. Endeavour has stopped.' James struck out with a will for the dinghy.

Sukhi sat waiting as the boat rocked and rolled, a trifle more than she liked, rising, and falling with the swell. She had watched James disappear into the night, and then the Endeavour, like an apparition, had done the same. It had felt as though she had been set adrift, until the line reached its limit, and she was lurched backwards, quite violently, by the tug of Endeavour.

The awful realization that James may have been killed and she was now stranded at sea without any idea of how to sail, or what direction to go even if she could make this thing move, was terrifying. She tried to remember his final instructions, 'Something about tilting the bow. No that's not it.'

Waves lapped up against the side and she looked for him, but there was nothing. And then, she shrieked, as he launched himself up and over the side and lay flat on his back trying to catch his breath. "Damn, that was a fucked-up plan."

***

"What just happened?" Engee's bodycam had shown everything, but Nathan was having trouble understanding.

An operative looked over the side rail, into the well. "He killed himself, sir."

Engee smiled. "Don't be an idiot. That was a perfect dive, and he had no shoes on. This was planned. Go to the bridge and tell the new captain I want to see him immediately." She turned her phone to face Nathan. "Don't worry sir, we will get him."

"Make sure you do. Alive, we need his tech."

"I'll make sure, sir."

Nathan signed off, and Butler came in at a run. Engee peered into the well. "Where does this go?"

"Out to the ocean. The science personnel use it to launch remote vehicles."

"Could a person use it to get out?"

"They'd have to be a strong swimmer. It would be dangerous. Someone pressed the deploying button and my bridge crew obeyed, slowing the ship."

"Does this Moore guy know what he's doing?"

"I don't know him that well — he's on the science side."

"If any of your crew have any inkling of our project they must go into the sea. If you don't report the truth, you will be the

95

next to go, and I will ensure your death is slow."

Butler had assessed the seriousness of the threat early and had adapted to the new order. "The crew and science team are completely isolated from one another. They have separate sleeping, eating and recreational facilities. The science team are like officers on this ship, whereas we are the enlisted crew, so to speak."

Engee got a clear read this was the truth. "Okay. Stop this ship, right now, and tell Gupta and the remaining science members to meet me in the captain's quarters."

Butler lifted his walkie-talkie, and as he walked off, he could be heard saying, "All stop, reverse engines, bring us to a full stop."

Chapter 21

Sukhi leapt up, almost capsizing the boat, and hugged James tightly. The tension and fear had been building for quite some time, she had passed her point of self-control and the relief at seeing him and realizing she was not going to be abandoned at sea, was overwhelming. "You took so long, James, I don't like the sea."

James hugged her and was about to answer when Endeavour lit up a huge swath of the ocean with her search lights. They both ducked down and stayed low. He whispered, knowing that sound could travel surprisingly far over water. "Without a mast, we should be hard to spot. But we must stay low."

He leaned over the side and put his hand in the sea. The ocean appeared deceptively calm with long lulls between larger wave sets. He was trying to gauge whether they, as the lighter craft, would be pushed to or from, the Endeavour.

His mind ran with a huge set of variables and calculations — time to daybreak, were they beyond the range of infrared, if he shipped the mast and attached the sail would they be seen, what would be the distance between them at daybreak, and would they be beyond the Endeavour's horizon — there were too many unknowns for an accurate assessment.

Engee had taken her sniper rifle to the observation deck and found a comfortable place to sit. She clipped on her thermal night-sight to the existing day scope, lifted it to eye level and swept a section of the ocean. It was a completely passive, micro-cooled mid-wave infrared technology that provided a high-resolution image — she peered through the sight and smiled, knowing she now owned the night.

James was now sure the distance between them, and Endeavour was closing and so he would have to run the risk and set sail, hoping they would not be seen. Sukhi watched him and could see the indecision. "I have no doubt you will come to the right decision."

"We have no choice; we must increase the distance between us." He threaded the mast into the sail cover, clipped on the boom, checked the rudder and daggerboard, and then they were on their way. He could feel through the rudder that she was a responsive, rigid, and reliable fiberglass boat. It had four watertight hull sections that could float independently and with bow waves breaking over them this felt safe, especially when he heard the self-bailer motor kick in to drain any water in the cockpit. He put her before the wind for maximum thrust and the speed was exhilarating — it felt good to be sailing again after all these years. He looked back and Endeavour was noticeably smaller. "Good."

Sukhi had stayed where he had told her she would be safe, and out of the way of the boom, which was good, as she was no sailor and feared the sea. She was looking ahead lounging peacefully, and as he hit the next wave it jarred the boat, and she flopped forward to reveal the large gaping exit wound in her head.

***

Phillip, Jo and Gupta entered the stateroom to find Engee in conversation with Butler.

"Follow, but do not hassle him into making a mistake. I need him alive."

"Yes... Excuse me, but do you prefer sir or madam?"

"Sir, today."

"Understood, sir," and he left.

She turned to Gupta. "Who are these people?"

"We had only five scientists left on board. Ajah, Moore, these two and myself."

Phillip felt this introduction was inadequate. "My name is Phillip Dressler — I'm the lead scientist on this vessel, and this is Josephine March, a post doc."

Gupta spoke up. "Dr Ajah has lacked all discretion. She believed Moore could solve this, so she forged a relationship to elicit his help. She prostituted herself, in my view."

Jo interjected. "Yes, he's right. She is, I'm sure, intimately involved with him."

"I have no need of these two. "How far along are you in solving the problem, Gupta?"

He cleared his throat. "I'm still in the preliminary phase of evaluation, but I do believe we can remedy the problems. It was my recommendation we do not begin human testing until all was verified with animals. But I was overruled."

"Ajah was the only one who had a plan we liked, but that appears to have gone awry. What do you know of Moore."

"He is an arrogant Englishman — particularly rude to me. Ajah was convinced his technology could tell us what was wrong, but I'm not convinced the man could come up with anything of real benefit."

Engee looked at Phillip and Jo. "You two must go. Gupta has stupidly mentioned too much, even now, making you both a liability. Unless you have something to offer?"

Gupta jumped to Jo's defense. "This young lady has been most helpful in complying with my wishes. She wants help with her research career. I could put her under my wing."

"Your new little pet Gupta? Ajah disappointed you, did she? No, she must go. She betrayed them, and she will betray us, just as easily."

Engee walked towards Jo and took her head in her hands, studying her face and eyes. She pleaded, "I'm a doctor, you can't do this, I'm a doctor..." and with a violent twist, Engee broke her neck.

She turned to Phillip, who had recovered enough from the shock to back away. He turned to Gupta and pleaded for him to intervene, but he was still looking with disappointment at Jo, and only momentarily glanced in his direction, lifting both hands and shrugging his shoulders to signal it was out of his hands. Phillip's eyes widened, and he tripped and fell back. Engee removed her throwing blade and climbed on top of him, and he swallowed to try and sound convincing. "Now, listen please, I can help you. I'm a member of a secret organization called The Collective. They have members everywhere, probably embedded in your organization, I'm sure. They were the people who told me to recruit James Moore. I can expose their agents, working as a double agent, so to speak." The moment he said the last sentence, he knew it was a mistake, as Jo had been killed for that very thing.

Engee placed her knife on his chest, and he grabbed her hands pushing it away with all his might, but she leaned forward using her body weight. "I have found people make up elaborate stories when they're faced with death, but rest assured, yours will go down as the most creative."

He pushed harder, but her height position gave her the advantage. "Please... please," he shouted but she inched the knife forward. "No, no listen," he said pleadingly as it pierced his skin and entered tissue. "Ahhh, I can help, I'm very important, I can give you what you need," he cried out in pain.

She pushed more and it punctured his heart. His eyes registered the shock, and he looked through her, offering up no further resistance and allowing the knife to slide in fully with no further obstruction.

Chapter 22

James was off the Aleutian Islands, tearing along at a fine pace. The rain blew sideways as he beat to windward and a burst of white water preceded a black shape that rose from the water, rolled over showing a scarred pectoral fin that seemed to wave, and then a dorsal fin, and finally a fluke before going under. James guessed she was a female, and she stayed with him companionably through the night.

His satellite phone had identified a charted reef about five miles ahead off Kilokak Rocks, which was where he was heading, and he was surprised she had followed him so far into shallow waters — it must be deeper than the hydrographic soundings given.

The Endeavour had maintained her distance, which James had tested by changing speed, exposing their desire not to press an engagement until they were ready. He had wrapped Sukhi in sail cloth in the night and placed her carefully in the cabin. His mind had told him he could gain a few extra knots if he had buried her at sea, but it felt wrong and he dismissed the idea.

The whale breached, almost intentionally washing spray right across his bow, waking him from melancholy thoughts. It felt like a signal, and he searched the surrounding sea to find Endeavour had narrowed the gap quickly and launched a jet ski with two riders. It peeled away from the rear and was coming on fast. He had expected this, picked up his satellite phone, and activated a preset program.

Engee and Butler were on the bridge watching this play out through binoculars. "This is your best driver, captain?"

"Yes sir. He has many, many hours of experience."

The jet ski went airborne as it leapt over rollers and the operative tightly gripped the two handles, unsure as to why this pilot needed to drive so fast. They were about three cable lengths from the sailing boat, and the man they chased, who had become such a high priority to capture, was just staring at them eating something, but doing nothing to get away. 'Maybe he has had enough of this rough sea and endless rain and welcomes the idea of being caught and taken back to the warm ship.'

Engee watched as the gap narrowed and smiled relishing the thought of continuing her conversation with this man, who seemed to think as she did. From this distance it looked as though they were right on him, and then the jet ski flipped and spun flinging its occupants off with great force. They splashed down and there was no movement from either.

"What just happened, Butler?"

"It looks as though they hit something. Sonar, can you see anything?"

There was a pause as a crew member activated sonar and searched the way ahead. "Two ROVs, near the surface, trailing behind the sailing boat."

"Can you disable them?"

Another pause. "No sir, they appear to have some sort of lockout, but they are ours."

Butler turned to Engee. "He has two remote vehicles following behind him acting as a barrier. I will deploy the jet-drive boat to pick up our crew."

"Leave them. Have your boat chase and capture Moore avoiding these obstacles this time. Send two of your best and I will send two of my operatives."

"Yes sir." Butler went off to make all ready.

James was on the windward side of the island, but the mountain winds found him and accelerated him away from the shore. He tacked and made straight for a rocky shoal.

Asangis had been watching this chase play out from high on a hill and was surprised by James' move. Assuming he didn't know of the shoal, he waited for him to notice the white water and change course, but he didn't. He saw the jet boat launched from the rear of the ship and speed towards the tiny sailboat. Retrieving a small telescope from his pocket he trained it on the jet-drive boat and could see the occupants were heavily armed, and that the man in the sailboat was not. He felt an urge to help, but he was not in this life any more, and this was nothing to do with him.

He adjusted his focus and brought the man in the sailboat into close view. A white man, strong, but he must be stupid. He fine-tuned the focus and then she appeared again in the eyepiece: the white woman with the child, and she seemed to be beckoning him. He pushed the telescope shut and put it back in his pocket. He watched the idiot white man again — he handled the boat very well, a seasoned sailor, but how foolish to head straight onto the rocks. He must have seen them by now.

The jet-drive boat had two large motors, was gaining rapidly and would be on James in a moment. James reached the shoal, down came the sail, out he jumped dragging his low draft sail boat across the rocky prominence. Asangis watched as he stopped at a large boulder, lift out a package and place it in a natural rock cradle, and move on.

When the jet-drive boat arrived, they contemplated following but decided against it. They had been outmaneuvered, and so reluctantly had to retrace their way, to try and get around the prominence.

Asangis smiled at this clever evasion. The idiot white man was not looking like such a fool, after all. He watched as he got across the peninsular, leapt back in his boat, set his sail, and tacked away at speed.

Chapter 23

The aunts and Marianne were in the control room, gazing up at a large screen while Ferko and his team of about a dozen engineers were all at their control stations.

"We have been able to get exclusive satellite time from a Collective member. I'm bringing up the feed now." The screen blinked and the half crescent shape of the Aleutian Islands came into view. "Although he is out of service area, we can still trace James' phone and can now zero in on his position."

The feed zoomed in to show his sailing boat heading towards the rocky outcrop. They all watched as James outmaneuvered his pursuers and took off from the other side. Rose asked Ferko to zoom into James, and he could be seen leaning out to one side as his high-performance sailing boat picked up a headwind and he tacked quickly to run along the shore.

May made sounds of worry. "He looks tired Rose."

"He does May, but he's in his element. He was born of the sea — as a child he spent more time in it, than out of it. Ferko, can you zoom in on whatever he placed on that boulder?"

Ferko did and they all studied it. Ferko tried different angles, but it didn't make it easier. "I don't know what that is."

Marianne spoke up. "It's a dead body. He needed to lighten his load to get over the rocks quickly."

They were all quiet, and Marianne walked to the screen and asked Ferko to rewind back and zoom in on the pursuing boat. He did and they all saw the weapons held by the operatives.

Marianne had not finished. "Now sweep up to that hilltop and zoom in on that area, zoom in again, now zoom in on him." They all looked on at Asangis.

Marianne turned to Ferko. She was wearing a printed stretch-silk satin midi dress, platform satin sandals and mega U-link earrings. "How quickly can you get me there?"

Ferko considered. "Twenty-four hours."

Rose joined Marianne. "Try and make it sooner Ferko, he's in trouble." Rose smiled at Marianne and looked her in the eyes. "Beautiful dress Marianne," and she ran her hand over a small side pocket where she highlighted the outline of Marianne's pill container. "I understand, but we can't afford to lose you my dear. You are very important to us."

Tears welled up in her eyes, and she wiped them away quickly, still not used to the love from James' family. "It takes about two days to build up the level. I started yesterday."

"Go carefully my dear. We can send somebody else if you'd like?"

Marianne shook her head. "He saved me. He never judged me like so many others, and I will never forget all he did. I will not let anything happen to him — he has been through too much."

***

Asangis was on foot today as he had been hunting at the lower elevations, and he set off at a steady jog to watch this chase play out on the other side of his island.

James looked back once more at the body of Sukhi and made a promise to return and give her a proper burial. His whale companion happened to surface at this time and exhale a conical shaped spout of warm air and water droplets, that felt to him a farewell wave, and he reciprocated by raising his hand high and waving back in gratitude.

This side of the island had many V-shaped valleys created by the sheer-sided volcanoes and he surveyed these inlets to see which could best conceal his boat. He had been lucky with these two maneuvers at sea, but he had nothing else up his sleeve, and he knew all too well they would be on him shortly once they found a way around.

The wildlife was abundant. A black footed albatross had decided to shadow him, there were crested puffins, bears, goats scrambling up scraggy cliffs and caribou on the high hills. Looking up he could see the mountains in the mist, and thankfully a new mist was getting thicker, lifting off the sea and cutting down the visibility — it felt as though a storm was brewing. A small opening to a beach came into view, and inland he could see that the abundant fresh water had carved a deep ditch that might serve to conceal his boat.

He put almost everything in his backpack, sealed the boat with its cover and tied it off to two tree stumps. Needing to get to high ground he took off at a slow jog to reconnoiter. There were no trees, making him feel quite exposed, as the island's lower levels were covered with a luxuriant dense growth of herbage, shrubs and flowering plants.

Sea legs made for hard going at first, due to the illusion of self-motion, and as he climbed he came across peat bogs and ferns which gave more opportunities for cover. Looking back at the sea he could see no sign of the Endeavour or the jet-drive boat.

Tiredness was becoming an issue, as he had not slept for over twenty-four hours, and so he stopped at every high ridge to scour for a cave or some area that would serve as a shelter —

there was nothing. He found one of the stunted willow trees and sat with his back against the trunk, drained and deflated. Leaning his head back he must have sunk immediately into sleep, and then some higher sense alerted him to a threat, and this jarred him awake with a start, to come face-to-face with Asangis seated in front of him.

James leapt to his feet and backed away. This did not phase Asangis in the slightest, however, he merely looked troubled and asked, "Who is the small blonde, white woman holding the baby boy?"

James looked around searching for Helen. "She's my wife — where is she?"

"She is dead."

James dropped to his knees, the waking realization hitting him once again like a ton of bricks, and he could not stop himself from sobbing. These emotions had been held back for too long, and now they were out, they were not going to let go of him until he cried out a full measure.

Chapter 24

Engee sat with her six remaining operatives in the data collection conference room on board the Endeavour listening to a briefing from Butler, who pointed to the display to highlight his graphics.

"The Aleutians have fifty-seven volcanoes and are a chain of fourteen large and fifty-five small islands. This island is uninhabited and far out on the chain — it is twenty-five miles long and five miles across. Like the others, the terrain is rocky, mountainous, and barren. There is constant fog and rain, and at the high elevations snow. The highlands are alpine while the lowlands are wet tundra."

Engee looked irritated. "Keep to relevant facts. I don't want a geography lesson."

"Yes, of course. Fishing would have been his best bet for food but he has lost his boat now so he will more than likely gather edible plants, bird's eggs or hunt the abundance of land animals. The only dangerous animal for you, and him, will be the bears."

"Have you been able to spot him with any of the boat or helicopter patrols?"

"No, not so far. Discovering his boat confirmed he's on the island. The fog and rain cut down our visibility, which is why he must be ferreted out by a ground unit."

Engee pointed to a flat section of land on the map, just beyond the beach. "This will be our base camp. I want you to deliver two quads, and a trailer with a jet ski there, and enough fuel, tents, and supplies. Two of my operatives will stay on board to reinforce our lab security detail, and to ensure you don't run off."

Butler had the good sense to look confused, as though the thought had never occurred to him. Engee pointed to two operatives. "You two stay — any signs of an insurrection, kill the lot of them... you four are with me. We will run him down and capture him. He is of no value to us dead, so bring handguns and knives only for personal protection. Kill him by accident, and I will kill you."

***

James woke the following morning to the smell of cooking. He had followed Asangis blindly back to his home. Moments of extreme sorrow, numbness, guilt and of course anger had plagued him since Helen's death, and sobbing seemed to have deadened his feelings and dulled the pain. Looking around at this primitive underground hut he wondered why this man was living alone on this desolate island. He had a selection of weapons on a driftwood table nearby — a lance, harpoon, and spear throwers with darts.

Asangis handed him a bowl filled with some sort of fish, meat, and a vegetable. James thanked him and as he ate, he looked at a picture of a pretty young woman and a child, carefully preserved and framed in flowers hanging on the wall.

Asangis watched his eyes. "Do you like the food? It is sea urchin, arctic hare, and wild celery."

"Thank you, yes, it is very good."

"Your wife is persistent — she has appeared to me four times. You are not Russian?"

"No, I'm English. You speak very good English."

"Do you speak Aleut?"

"No, I'm sorry."

"It is a soft beautiful language; you cannot shout in Aleut." The wind howled above them. "The word for wind is like the sound of the wind 'sla-hooo.' Those people who are chasing you are landing and preparing to cover the island. But they hold back, they don't want to harm you. Why?"

"I have something they want, but they will use it for no good."

"They must be Russian."

"No, they are American."

"They are just as bad."

James noticed his clothes, boots, and the mittens were made from animal skins — they looked like sea lion or walrus. He had bird feathers in a hat, and they were all fur-lined. "What do you have against Russians?"

Asangis tucked into his food, and a long pause ensued. "My grandfather told us about them. They came to take whatever we had, but they wiped out a lot of my people."

"I'm sorry to hear that."

"One Russian commander, who was bored, wondered how many men a musket ball would travel through, so he lined up twelve Aleuts, fired, and found that it stopped at the ninth man. In another village they killed everyone except the young women to use on their voyage home and dropped them over the side when they sighted Russia."

"That is terrible, do Russians still come?"

"No, nobody comes, only broken Englishmen."

James looked again at the picture and Asangis followed his gaze. "I ran away to this island to mark time and die. There is no negative thinking in Aleut, no word for 'no' in our language... Yes, white man, we both lost a wife and child, and we both refuse to carry on."

112

Chapter 25

Captain Butler knocked on the door of the captain's state room and heard Engee call out, "Enter". She was sitting at a desk on a conference call she had paused and had changed from her fatigues and was wearing an off-white rucked T-minidress that clung to her figure so tightly it left very little to the imagination. Her feet were crossed and high on the desk showing pearl platform sandals and she twisted her long auburn hair wig with one hand.

"Yes, captain?"

"We have landed all the equipment and supplies you requested. A heavy storm is coming in, so I didn't know if you wanted to bring back your operatives. The weather should be better tomorrow, sir, I mean ma'am."

"Bring back two, and tell the other two to maintain six hour watches. We cannot leave our base camp unattended."

"Understood ma'am."

Engee continued her call with Nathan. "All is in hand; we should have him by tomorrow."

Nathan paused. "I miss my little bunny. Show me what you're wearing."

Engee stood up twisting, turning, and bending provocatively. Nathan made appreciative noises, and then he was interrupted. "I must go. Get it done and get back as soon as you can with the package."

"Of course, sir."

Nathan smiled and gave a little wink before disconnecting.

Engee sat down, removed her wig, and fingered her short hair into place before making another call. She was connected to a nursing home and put through to an infirm lady sitting in a winged chair being attended to by a nurse and an orderly. They placed a tablet in front of her and she smiled at seeing Engee. "I'm so glad you called Peter."

Engee's voice lowered. "How are you mother?"

"Wonderful my dear boy. They look after me so beautifully here. I do hope it is not too expensive?"

"Not at all."

Her mother turned the tablet to the nurse. "This is my son, Peter. He is a top executive you know. Very important." The nurse smiled and said hello, and Engee waved in return.

"It has been a while since you visited. Can you come soon?"

"Next week for sure. I'm out of town at the moment."

The mother announced this to her attendants. "He travels the world you know."

"I do have to go now mother. I have an early start tomorrow."

"I understand, get a good night's sleep. Peter?"

"Yes mother."

"Have nothing to do with your sister, she is always trouble."

Engee did not answer but looked off to the side.

"I mean it son; she is a freak of nature. Makes up stories. Everyone is always against her, trying to hurt her. It's ridiculous."

"She isn't so bad mother. I was there when those boys attacked her after the football game."

"Don't mention that again Peter. She made it all up for attention. She is an abomination of the Lord. Stay away from her, she'll only be trouble."

"Okay mother."

"You were hurt so badly protecting her. The doctors said you would never recover, never wake again. And look at you now. I bet they felt silly."

Engee smiled and nodded. "All better now."

***

The storm ravaged the Aleutians, that necklace of islands birthed from hundreds of now drowned volcanoes. It arrived at Asangis' island lashing the western tip with winds of sixty miles per hour in the early evening, causing Endeavour to seek refuge from the thirty-foot waves. Visibility dropped to eighteen feet, and eight inches of snow fell on his home in the mountains.

Asangis handed James some wet weather gear and began to dress in his own. "You will need to even the odds with a raid."

"Now?"

"No better time. I can walk this island blindfolded, and with this storm we will be blind... but then, so will they."

Asangis picked up a spear thrower and four spears and slung them onto his back.

James questioned, "Do we need weapons?"

"They have them."

"Can we just disable them?"

"They don't want to harm you, but they won't think twice about killing me. I will avoid bloodshed, if possible, but these people have killed before and will think nothing of it. I will die one day, but my spirit is harmed if I injure myself on purpose."

"What do you intend?"

"I like fires. They purify evil, and I can sense bad spirits."

James stopped dressing and looked at him. "Why are you helping me?"

"We have an old saying. Help someone good and good things happen; help someone bad and bad things happen."

"How do you know I'm good?"

"My wife told me to help your wife, and your wife told me to help you... do English people always talk so much?"

James smiled and they were off.

The visibility was very poor, and James lost all sense of direction very quickly. Asangis had given him a cord to hold, and he followed behind, head down. A glow appeared in the distance and Asangis told James to get on his knees and crawl. They got very close and could see the camp now, and a guard walking the perimeter.

Asangis came close so they could speak, and he waited for James to say something. "Do you have a plan?"

"A diversion of some type?"

Asangis smiled. "I can see why your wife nagged me... You walk forward in exactly ten minutes and act as though you are going to give yourself up. I will circle around and start a fire near the gas tanks. When it blows, run back into the night and I will find you."

James liked it — it was simple and clean. "I understand. Thank you again Asangis."

He nodded, smiled, patted James on the shoulder and disappeared into the night. At the appointed time James began to walk forward calling out with his hands in the air. The guard did not hear him above the howling wind and continued his patrol. James shouted louder, and he still went unnoticed. When he was very close, he shouted again startling the guard, who spun around in a panic, drew his gun, and started shooting wildly. James threw

116

himself to the ground and when he looked up a slender shadow seemed to pass through the guard's body, and he dropped to his knees and fell face down into the dirt.

The shooting woke the other guard, and he came out half-dressed shooting in all directions. One of these shots must have hit a gas tank, because there was an almighty bang and the night sky lit up like daylight for a few seconds, long enough for James to see Asangis, knees bent and feet spread shoulder-width apart, raise his throwing arm to eye level, start a forward throwing action like a pitcher throwing a fast ball, and flick his wrist forward at the end of the throw to add momentum and leverage to the spear. The passage of the spear was rapid, could hardly be traced, and like the other guard it passed straight through his body, and he fell in a slump still shooting into the air.

Asangis retrieved his two spears as he returned to James, offered him a hand, and pulled him up laughing. "Well, that was not the plan, but it worked!"

Chapter 26

On their return Asangis had coated the right of his face with sea lion fat, having been singed by the explosion, and went to bed. He hugged James before retiring and could be heard laughing involuntarily as he replayed the raid in his mind.

James sat waiting, and if the truth be told, he still hoped to have an encounter with Helen and their son. Asangis had the good fortune of seeing her four times, and this could not be dismissed as his description of her was perfect. Her spirit was here in this desolate place, but why? And why was he not afforded an encounter? After she died, he had needed to see her and this had become desperate, building to an intensity in which he pleaded for one last goodbye.

He opened his journal in hopes that writing to her, and so putting her in the forefront of his mind, might trigger her appearance. It was all so unreal now thinking back to the funeral. People had struggled with what to say and he had forced himself to cry alone beforehand in hopes of keeping himself together for the ordeal. People offered up the usual platitudes of condolence, of course, and then after the funeral they appeared to struggle with what to say and how to help someone who could not be helped, and so they avoided him.

'I'm sorry you lost her'… It was such a strange expression. It implied he had accidentally left her at the shopping mall — but it was much more violent than that. It should have been, 'I'm sorry you had such a vital element severed from your heart and mind.' He had run away to the mountains, found a ranch and a home that felt like a long-lost friend, been joined by JP, such a dear friend, and horses — those beloved animals with their warm hearts and loving kindness. 'I need to go home.'

He opened his journal and to his shock there was a note written to him from Sukhi...

Dear James,

I waved goodbye to you just moments ago and you disappeared into the night, and here I am sitting alone in a small boat in the middle of this huge ocean, and I'm scared to death. I found some clothes as you told me to, and found this journal, and having morbid thoughts I decided to write down what I needed to tell you.

For some reason I feel as though death is close at hand, and it seems important to tell you how much I have fallen in love with you, and how our time together has been so wonderful. I'm well aware, you have not fallen in love with me. I didn't know this journal had letters to your wife and son — I stopped reading them as soon as I realized. Please forgive me for using it but nothing else is available.

I do need to document my inner thoughts on this project that I wish I had never been a part of. My theory is that during REM sleep the brain performs a vital function of defragmentation. The events of the day occur randomly, and these disorganized or fragmented memories have to be collated otherwise the strain put on the brain to access these jumbled parts will cause memory recall and dementia issues. Defragmenting simply organizes the contents of our mind so that memories are stored in the smallest number of contiguous regions. I believe that is the vital function that is happening when we go into REM sleep — dreams play

119

back past and recent memories as it sorts them out. Dream Degree prevents REM sleep, leaving memories fragmented, overloading our brains' processor resulting in psychosis and hallucinations. This was my line of investigation and I believed your Mind-Link system could uncover whether this was true.

My education has severely limited my possibility of finding a husband and having a family, since none of my prior boyfriends wanted a partner that was smarter than they were. I tried to pretend to be dumb, a little girl lost, but that was not me, and they seemed to know that. I so hope you appear soon as I'm giving up hope. If you do not, I'll be adding to this letter, much the same as you have been writing to your wife. I hear a noise so I will sign off.

I do love you James,
Sukhi xx

***

Asangis shook James awake, the journal still open on his chest. "We pissed them off. The weather has lifted and they're in their helicopter buzzing the island, looking in every nook and cranny. We must go."

It was the dogs that gave them away, as the noise of the helicopter activated their guarding instincts, and they abandoned their naturally made igloos to bark at their approach.

Engee pointed out Asangis and James exiting the sub level home and readying the sled. James climbed into the basket and the dogs were off, tearing along in response to encouraging calls from Asangis.

James had expected the dogs to all be uniform in shape and size, but genetics had been mixed to breed a rag tag group that

120

was hardy, fast and had high endurance. They stretched out with such athleticism, and the pace ramped up, made to feel even faster by kicked up snow and because they were so close to the ground. James looked up and the helicopter turned to make a run at the sled and James could see a rifle barrel extend out ready. He turned in his seat, laid back and pointed a handgun he had taken the night before. Asangis saw this and kneeled a little to give James a clear view. James took careful shots, but the moving sled made him highly inaccurate. One did ricochet off the fuselage and this forced the pilot to peel off and come in again.

They used a different tactic this time, staying at a distance where the rifle was effective, but the handgun was not. It was an automatic rifle and a burst took down three dogs at once, the sled toppled and tumbled throwing its occupants out.

Asangis was knocked out, James staggered to his feet, and could not find the handgun. He ran off to lower ground where the snow had melted, trying to draw them away from Asangis. They followed in the helicopter, and he was so busy keeping them in sight he almost went straight off a high cliff — he was trapped.

The helicopter landed, and out stepped Engee and two operatives, who diverged away in opposite directions to take up a triangular position. Engee was in her fatigues and smiled at his predicament. "Mr Moore, we have you; can we stop these games."

121

Chapter 27

Engee walked forward to take lead position flanked either side by her heavily armed operatives. "You are all alone Mr Moore."

Asangis appeared with a limp and a cut on his forehead to stand by James. "He is not alone."

James hugged him. "I tried to keep you out of this."

Asangis smiled. "You are a good man, and that is why your spirit team won't stop."

Engee pulled her throwing knife from its sheaf at the back of her neck. "Cooperate and we will spare your friend."

Asangis leaned in to James. "Why is she so pissed off?"

"She whacked a log with a blunt axe all day, and then someone suggested that if she sharpened the axe she could cut right through it, and did you know what she answered?"

"What?"

"But then I'd have to find another log."

Asangis nodded, liking the analogy.

A choppy heavy wind could be heard from below the cliff line, and they wondered if it was the storm returning, but it had a regular repeating pattern. A commercial black hawk helicopter lifted behind James and Asangis and landed alongside them, and out stepped Marianne. She walked quickly to James and kissed him on both cheeks in the European manner and then hugged him tight lifting up one leg. He responded, so pleased to see her. Asangis watched this exchange with interest, and when James introduced him as his very good friend, Marianne grabbed him too giving him hugs and cheek kisses.

Her make-up was '70s inspired, with thick artificial eyelashes and layers of teal eye shadow. She had psychedelically colored platform boots, a very short, tightly-knit teal miniskirt, cinched around her waist with a highly decorative belt with the letter 'M' in its buckle, and a pale-blue zip-up sweater that was tight and unzipped to show a beautiful bosom. She took up a playful pose in front of James and Asangis, facing Engee, teasing her long black hair with her fingers. "What have we here?"

Engee could feel the strength and confidence coming off Marianne, she noticed the expensive helicopter and was trying to understand how James seemed to have people always coming to his rescue. "My business is with him, not you."

Marianne tilted her head to size up Engee and looked at the throwing knife in her hand. "Why don't you pick on someone your own size."

With practiced precision Engee flipped her knife, caught the blade, lifted it to eye level and threw it hard for speed. Marianne snatched it effortlessly from the air, and in a backspin slide-slung the blade at one operative where it wedged in his neck. Despite her boots she leaped onto him as he fell, pulled the knife from his neck and threw it hard almost from behind killing the other operative and as he dropped to his knees, while trying to remove the blade from his throat, Marianne reached for it and withdrew it so that it slit his throat completely. Engee had decided that discretion was the better part of valor, backing away from this.

Marianne toyed with the blade. "A pretty little knife, very well balanced," and then with a rapid reflex threw it back at Engee, who, like Marianne, caught it in mid-flight. It stung in her hand; the throw was aimed at her face, and as much as she tried to conceal it, she had to shake out the sting.

Marianne smiled at seeing this. "I like knives, but it is time for you to leave in your little bitty helicopter."

Engee turned to leave but paused as if to reconsider. Marianne reached for her 'M' shaped handle in her belt buckle, and half pulled out a tri-blade knife. "I will give you no quarter."

Engee walked away with as much composure as she could muster and left in her helicopter.

Marianne turned and jumped on James and then started to check him all over to see he was not harmed. "Aunt Rose and May will never forgive me if I failed. They are waiting for our call."

Asangis watched all of this in confusion, and when James gave him a questioning look, he turned to James with a smile. "Saved by a girl... I have never been more humiliated!"

***

Saying farewell to Asangis had proved to be quite difficult for James and he had delayed it under the guise of not being quite ready. It was strange how a chance encounter and significant shared experience made it so hard to say goodbye. He kept thinking they were like ships passing in the night, and that made it even more painful, as he wanted him to be a more permanent part of his life.

Asangis felt James' difficulty and understood it. "You have a chance James, at a second life, and you should take it. After my wife and child died, I felt the decline in me as though I was falling into a pit, and I could not stop it as I clawed for solid ground." He motioned to Marianne, who was hovering not too far away from them. "She loves you..."

James interrupted. "Marianne? Oh no. I helped her, and so

what you're seeing is gratitude."

Asangis laughed. "Send me a message on this phone you gave me when the two of you are married."

"Honestly, Asangis, we are just friends."

"Our people are hunters and warriors and this we understand. When she fought, it was personal. She killed those men and provoked that woman because they threatened you."

James looked off at Marianne who was playing with Asangis' new puppies. He had lost three dogs, but a female had given birth to five — the pack would be restored.

"I know how you think James because you are me a year ago. You think no one will ever love you as she did, and you believe you cannot be loved again. But a new love will save you... Find someone to love before it's too late."

James listened, unused to someone seeing him so clearly, but knowing he was well qualified to speak. He knew he was right, had felt the decline, and knew, sooner or later, what was left to be got, wouldn't be worth getting. Asangis chuckled to himself.

"What are you thinking Asangis?"

He was staring at Marianne. "I was thinking of what your sex will be like, with this one. I should imagine it will be quite... vigorous!"

Chapter 28

Nathan waited on the patio of his beachfront home, and Engee was shown through by a maid. She was truly gender-neutral today with a classic white button-down dress shirt, paired with slim fit boyfriend jeans, and accessorized with a simple metal bar necklace. Nathan looked on at her with pleasure but reined in his ardor. "Usual?"

"Yes please."

The maid left and returned with a scotch and soda. The covered brick patio overlooked sand dunes and a tidy stand of palm trees that sloped down to the Pacific, where you could hear the rhythm of waves breaking on the shore. She took a seat opposite and crossed her legs with an ankle-on-knee pose that portrayed relaxation, and then gave the highlights of her trip.

Nathan paused, sat back, and took a sip of his drink. "So, he performs an apparent suicide dive, has pre-planned his escape taking Sukhi with him, runs to an island where he had a built-in native-American warrior who was willing to die for him, and then wonder woman shows up and kills two of my elite guards easily with your knife... Who is this guy? "

"I don't know."

"Is he Illuminati?" he said with a scoff. "He seems too well connected, as though he's a member of some secret organization."

Engee reflected on this as it resonated strongly with the story Dressler had told her in hopes of gaining a reprieve from execution. This piece of intelligence she decided to omit.

"What about the rest of it — all clean?"

"Yes. We were fortunate with the violent storm. It threatened shipping in the area and so no one was surprised Endeavour went down with all hands, two other fishing vessels were lost without a trace. The crew and the new captain helped to scuttle the ship, making it appear natural, assuming I would let them live as they had followed orders so obediently. Their look of shock when they were killed was priceless."

"Good… you know Sukhi was our best hope at fixing this. Gupta is an idiot. And she believed the technology James Moore came up with would help us identify the problem."

"That's true. It all went to plan; she reported getting close to him and then something went wrong."

"Where is he now?"

"He returned to his ranch in the mountains of San Diego."

"Hmm… We need to do our homework and approach him differently. Get the AI group involved, maybe they can devise an approach with a high probability of success."

"Yes sir."

"We can't wait too long. Two weeks max. Containment on this end has been problematic and the rumor mill is already in play. We are using all our influencer connections at present to counter and confuse. Let him relax and settle and then we will head back in."

Engee nodded agreement.

Nathan got up and walked towards her and sat at her feet. "Bunny?"

Engee put down her drink and slapped him across the head. He immediately cowed but said nothing. "Get in that room and take everything off. I want to see that puny little body of yours."

***

Knowing he would be monitored, James opted to go to the ranch, unwilling to lead them to his aunts in Switzerland. Marianne insisted on staying close at hand as there was still a clear and present danger.

They sent word ahead to JP, and they arrived at the ranch tired and hungry from a long day of travel. They were welcomed by the heavenly aroma of his cooking and as he appeared from the kitchen, apron on and all smiles, he could not conceal his relief at seeing James in one piece. He had not met Marianne before but had been told all, and he hugged Marianne first. "Thank you for bringing him home safe and sound Marianne. Trouble seems to follow him."

JP was unfamiliar with the European style of greeting and his head collided with Marianne's when she swapped to kiss his other cheek. To conceal his embarrassment and not seem unresponsive, he continued the cheek-to-cheek kissing well past the customary two, which produced a giggle from Marianne and a smile from James. When she was released, she placed a hand on James' arm. "People are drawn to him. They know he's a kind soul who can solve their problems."

"Thank you, Marianne, what a nice thing to say."

Their eyes met and JP studied this covertly, and then returned to the kitchen calling back, "Get changed you two, I've laid the table on the patio."

As they walked off, James pointed down the hallway. "This way. Your case is being sent on?"

Marianne replied with a coy expression, "Cases… there are a few."

"I should have guessed! I had noticed you like your clothes. You always look very nice, by the way."

"Thank you. This house is beautiful, it feels so European. There is something safe about things that have been around for centuries."

"You're right, I'm glad you like it. I will lend you some of my things this evening and take you to the feed store to get you some gear tomorrow. Would you like to go horse riding?"

Marianne linked her arm in his as they walked. "Oh, yes please James! I have never been."

James was first on the patio and found JP making it picture perfect. Flowering vines crawled up a log arbor surrounding this small island dining area that looked out to the mountains of Jamul — each of which James knew very well, like old friends. The simple laid-back furniture complemented the overall feel and beauty of the property. A stone fireplace contained burning logs, and a crisply ironed tablecloth and floating candle added to the richly layered atmosphere as the afternoon stretched into evening.

JP appeared with two glasses of white wine. "Oh, she's not here yet?"

"I left her in my closet to choose whatever she wanted... You certainly went to town JP — thank you. It's good to be home."

"I knew you'd had a rough time of things, and so..." JP stopped speaking mid-sentence, and as James turned to find out why, he followed his gaze to Marianne as she approached.

She had selected a zipped semi-distressed sweat-shirt jacket opened to reveal one of his graphic t-shirts tied in a corner knot to reduce its size, loose sweat-shirt pants, and white socks. These were his things, and yet they looked entirely different on her. It was strange how comfortable she looked, and how much that put him at ease. Her figure, which he knew to be toned and curvy, was now concealed, and yet the more it was hidden the more his mind worked to identify it whenever she stretched or leaned.

JP worked in the kitchen like an artist worked in oils. It was a late life calling for him, and he had reached a point where he was able to imagine the flavor he wanted, and simply mix the ingredients to achieve it. "I knew you'd be hungry. I wouldn't serve airline food to our pigs! By the way, those piglets are the noisiest critters on the farm, they outdo that damned rooster."

Marianne looked at James and her face lit up. "Piglets — I must see them!"

"I will introduce you to them tomorrow — there are five boys and two girls."

"What a life. What made you choose it?"

"After Helen died, I wanted to get away, and this is about as far away as you can imagine. But it resonated with my soul, and so I'm not running away any more. I'm exactly where I should be."

JP delivered grilled bread, brushed with olive oil, and sprinkled with salt, with chopped spicy tomatoes and cheese.

James continued, "It is so very different to the fishing village I grew up in, but life slows down up here to a slow walk. I rescued a horse called Cora, and she bridged a connection with horses I never knew existed. My grandfather, Jack, a very wise man, was in India with the British army and he had a horse he never stopped talking about. He was quite boring on the subject, really. I know now what he meant — I want you to meet Cora tomorrow. She's exceptional."

"But you don't ride Cora, you ride another horse, called, 'em…"

"John-Henry, yes, Cora was never trained, and it would just feel wrong."

"I want to meet her. I hope she likes me."

"She will like you because she will read you. Horses have such high empathy — they read your mind. If I think it, they respond the same way as though I've said it... Thank you for helping me, Marianne."

JP bustled in with risotto, made with chicken broth, and then freshly caught trout, baked with lemon, green beans with almonds and a baked potato, changing wines, of course.

James acknowledged this. "Thanks JP, I can't tell you how much we're enjoying it."

When he left, Marianne looked up from her food and caught his eyes. "You are so different to any man I have ever known. You never judged me, always helped me. I never understood why."

"You're a good person Marianne. They conditioned you to believe you weren't, but we must unravel that, so you can discover who you are and who I see — a beautiful person who loves deeply."

JP's timing was impeccable, and he came out, oblivious. "Okay, this is guinep fruit, queso fresco, cheddar, and a spiced cheese, and where would you be without fresh ground and brewed coffee, with cream... Oh, and I made some press sugar cookies."

Marianne's watch chimed and she reached for a pill box and stopped. James knew exactly what that meant. "No Marianne, you mustn't."

"I only take the pain blocker, not the empathy blocker. I want to make the most of our time together."

"Why did you do it Marianne?"

131

Marianne paused for a moment. "I did it for you, James."

James held her eyes and it touched him deeply.

True to form, JP walked in holding two liqueur glasses filled with Kahlua. "You may have noticed I followed the Italian seven course meal structure this evening," he said proudly, and realized he may have committed a faux pas. "Although now I think of it, I should have chosen the French."

Marianne came to the rescue. "It was perfect, so welcome. Thank you, JP."

James added, "Couldn't have been better."

JP looked down at his notes. "They mentioned to finish off with a liqueur but only if they're staying over. Not if they're driving. So, you two are okay to have it."

James couldn't decide whether an answer was necessary but did all the same. "Yes, we won't be driving."

JP studied his notes, again. "Okay, one more thing. It also asks you to answer this question, so you can think about it. What is your idea of a romantic evening?"

JP looked to the two of them pencil in hand, James paused for only a moment before answering. "One that is not planned."

Chapter 29

Marianne decided the feed store was too limited but found a chic fashion boutique called Rodeoware in La Jolla, and so they went on a shopping spree. James sat and watched with pleasure as she modeled rodeo-ready raw denim jeans that looked as though they were painted on, paisley-printed prairie dresses, jean midi-skirts, but he noticed she never changed a pair of bedazzled black-and-white cowboy boots. She accessorized with all styles and colors of cowboy hats, western-inspired shirting and fringe jackets.

"I cannot decide what to get James, it is all so beautiful."

He said teasingly, "I noticed you're not sure about those kinky boots."

She smiled and kissed him, "I love these boots, and we will never be parted!"

"Let's get the lot. That way you can fill your closet at the ranch. You look so good in everything."

She came close to him and looked at him directly. She had big brown eyes and they probed him intently. "Why were you never scared of me? Did I intimidate you. Men say I intimidate them."

"You did, a little, but I could see you had a good heart."

"Men saw me in only two ways, but not you. You can read me like I can read you."

James felt the weight of her stare reach deep inside him, and he let it. Marianne was a mimic savant, abandoned by her parents, and weaponized from childhood. Her handlers had her take chemical blockers to null her pain receptors so she wouldn't be disabled if she was hurt, and block her empathy so she had no feelings for her opponent. She smiled. "You are not intimidated by me."

"I like your strength and conviction, but I see your vulnerability and sadness. You are a good person, Marianne."

"Coming from you, I think I could believe that."

James put his arms around her waist. "What two ways?"

"They saw me as unstable, or… as porn."

"That is not how I see you, and that is not who you are. I can read you, and you know who you are."

"I see that, maybe… it is possible?"

James smiled at her and pulled her closer. "Impossible n'est pas Francais!"

***

Marianne went with James to meet his horses. The two boys, John-Henry and Kai were horsing around at the far end of the pasture. Kai was a young paint gelding James had been training, a safe and steady ride who didn't have the stamina yet, but he was such a sweet and gentle soul.

Cora appeared to sense the two of them before they were even in sight, as she was waiting by the rail staring, still finishing a mouth full of alfalfa. She was a light chestnut quarter horse with a lucky white patch on her forehead, slender but muscular, a little smaller than John-Henry, maybe fourteen hands from the withers — and this made her distinctively feminine. She whinnied as they approached, and Marianne slipped between the rails as though she had been told to. Cora approached her and they touched, and James thought it strange how he was completely ignored. Cora led her off and for an hour they stayed together leaning in on each other.

James knew what was happening because the same thing had happened to him. He was leaving the feed store and there was her photo, and a sign that read, 'date to slaughter'. It was the very next day, and a panic overwhelmed him and he made call after call until he was assured she had been saved and that he could adopt her. He had saved her, and then they had met, and it was all at once unclear as to who had saved whom.

Horses offer a safe space to reveal emotional pain. You build a relationship of trust in which they offer a sense of peace with no threat of bias or judgement. Like Marianne, horses are keen observers, vigilant and highly sensitive, and mirror your emotion with understanding. Cora would immediately sense Marianne's vulnerability and encourage her to open up about emotional challenges and past traumas that were too painful to speak of, and by externalizing these feelings it would make it easier to broach them again and process them through.

They rode for most of the day, James on John-Henry and Marianne on Kai. For someone who had never ridden before, she handled Kai perfectly, and when he asked how she did it, she explained she was simply mimicking him. She would frequently lean forward and cuddle Kai around the neck, but Kai seemed to like it and James could see him taking care of her.

JP had packed a lunch basket with a flask of hot coffee, a bottle of white Zinfandel, and ever-roast chicken sandwiches with a selection of fruit. James took her to a shady spot near a seasonal stream. They ate, drank, laughed, and dozed in the sun. James watched her lying there and realized he had fallen in love.

She lifted a hand to shade her eyes. "What?"

James shook his head and smiled.

135

"Tell me, you look embarrassed."

"When I was younger, they insisted on teaching us poetry, the classics. It was so removed, so disconnected I had felt it was a waste of time and paid little attention. The death of Helen and our son cut so deeply, and as I traveled trying to find out where I belonged, parts of these poems came back so clearly, as though my life now resonated with the poets — I found out I was not alone."

Marianne's eyes filled with tears. "I remember when you left. I wanted so much to help you... to take you off, and somehow make you whole again."

James put his hand in hers.

"What poem came to you at that time?"

"It is very sad."

"Tell me."

"It is Housman... 'That is the land of lost content, I see it shining plain, the happy highways where I went, and cannot come again.'"

Tears dropped from her eyes, and he wiped them away. "But that is not what I was thinking when I was looking at you."

"What were you thinking?"

"It is a Shelley poem."

"Tell me."

He was reluctant.

"Please tell me."

"'And the sunlight clasped the earth, and the moonbeams kissed the sea, but what are all these kissing's worth, if thou kiss not me?'"

Marianne leaned up. "I've been waiting for you."

James lowered his head to hers, still a little hesitant... and they kissed.

Chapter 30

Living on a farm seemed to give you more time in each day. Marianne was up early with James and out to feed, water and muck-out the animals. This was such a departure from the hustle and bustle of before and it felt as though she had stepped outside of her old life and was now living in an alternate universe. She had always had a deep connection with animals and now she lived amongst all manner of them in all stages of growth and had even helped in the birth of two baby Pygmy goats.

She now realized how much time she had spent in the past cooped up indoors, due to the stark contrast of farm life and communing with nature which drew her outside for most of the day. It was hard work, and she had thrown herself into this agricultural lifestyle cleaning out the greenhouse and planting tomatoes, potatoes, several herbs, grapes, and a mango and several avocado trees. She was naturally a quick study, and JP had been teaching her how to cook, the meals of which put fine dining to shame. Her world was filled with simple pleasures, like finding out that nothing compared to cooking an egg from your own chicken.

The sound of silence in the mountains was mesmerizing, and she could finally hear herself think. A breeding pair of hawks had nested nearby and their high pitched 'kee-arr' went straight to her soul, and she knew her life was more complete for having heard it. Waking up with James and having coffee on the veranda in their robes, listening to the early calls from the animals, and seeing the marine layer that rolled in overnight isolating them and their mountain from the rest of the world — it was beyond words. It brought her well and truly into the here and now. Previously, she had spent most of her time reflecting on her traumatic past or wishing away time hoping for a better future — she now lived firmly in the present, and the privacy and seclusion had secured for her such peace and happiness.

She was brushing down Cora and was pulled out of these thoughts when she became aware James was watching her, with a knowing smile. "Yes, mon amour?"

He walked to her and whispered, even though there was nobody for miles around. "You were wonderful last night, my love."

"You were too. It is so perfect when you love someone, it goes so deep."

James smiled at this last word, and was about to say something inappropriate, but was playfully admonished. "James!"

He took her in his arms. "You said you had something you wanted to do today?"

"Yes, if you don't mind."

"Anything, my love."

"Well, my cases arrived yesterday, and I have three new bikinis I need to try…"

"I'm loving this idea, already!"

"Now listen… are all Englishmen such wonderful lovers!"

James tried to adopt a serious demeanor. "Yes, we are instructed in this art form in the final term of our finishing school."

"You are such a nit wit! Getting back to my question, when we got satellite time we found you on a sailing boat, tearing along

— it looked so exhilarating, and I thought, I'd love to do this with you."

"Go sailing?"

"Yes, if possible?"

"Yes, of course. You are in luck because JP has a friend who moors his yacht at the Coronado sailing club, and he never minds if I take it out for some exercise. There is one condition."

"James," she said sternly, knowing full well he could not be serious.

"You have to pose for me in all three bikinis."

"That I will do, although they are itty-bitty things that barely cover me."

James put his head in his hands, his imagination running wild, and keen for what was in store he took her by the hand and made quickly for the house. "We should leave immediately!"

***

The friend of JP's was happy to oblige; they packed overnight bags and a store of food and were off, heading south in the 'Surprise', a fast, seaworthy, and sweet-lined twenty-five-foot sloop. There was such freedom in sailing and James had always reveled in it. You could chart your own course and so choose your adventure, which in this case was to run down to Baja and anchor overnight in a cove.

Marianne lay on the deck forward, the wind picking up her hair under a pink baseball cap. She turned her head back towards James, tipped down her sunglasses to show her eyes and smiled at him, soaking up this experience as another wave broke over the bow sending back a fine spray. She wore an impossibly tiny teal bikini that popped against her tanned complexion. Always

139

working out with a purpose, she kept herself fighting fit, and this was clear in her athletically toned figure. The cups barely contained her chest, and the cut pulled in to create a lovely cleavage. The lower half was also skimpy and only covered what was necessary, with a thin waistband that sat high on her hips accentuating her trim flat midsection.

Marianne joined James at the wheel. "Now my love, tell me what I need to know."

James knew that when she switched on in this way, she soaked up information like a sponge and forgot nothing. It was strange, as this accelerated learning is what Brainwave was trying to master.

She was staring at him. "You are thinking about them?"

"Yes. They won't go away of their own accord."

"I agree. I have been thinking about it too and believe it is better for us to go to them than let them come to us."

"I like that plan."

"How is this boat actually working?"

"The aerodynamic forces of the wind act on the sails and these combine with the hydrodynamic forces of the water, to propel it forward. Sailboats would slide sideways with the wind if they did not have a centerboard or keel under the hull."

"I see, interesting." Marianne was able to watch a concert pianist play a piece and immediately mimic it. For this reason, James did not hold back from the details.

"Stability and ballast keep a sailboat from capsizing. The keel is typically weighted with lead to keep it in the water. The angle of the sail can be adjusted to efficiently capture the wind, and this is normally different to the direction your boat is heading."

"I understand, may I take the wheel?"

"Yes, you will feel the forces as they play on the rudder."

"I feel it, yes... So, what is our next step?"

"I made a call to Rose, and they have a Collective member in the executive branch of Brainwave. He is reporting on all developments. I told her we were going away for two days, and we would call on our return."

Marianne smiled. "Has she guessed do you think?"

"I think Rose knew long before we did!"

Marianne knew this to be true and smiled. "What are you going to offer them?"

"Sukhi's theory is a very good one. They should pursue it."

"Would that be enough? They want the Mind Link."

"Yes, but they can't have it. Technology is generally designed for good intentions, the internet was so scientists could share their findings collaboratively, but it is eventually abused and used negatively. People like this would exploit it immediately."

Marianne was looking at the shoreline. "So, this is why you keep sailing in a zig zag, instead of just following the coast line?"

"Yes. Working the sails, fighting the sea elements and the weather, this is what makes sailing so stimulating — it's a continuous mental challenge to optimize for best results."

"When we get back let's get a full briefing from Ferko, and then make contact... That is the most beautiful coastline."

James put his arms around her waist. "It's the Baja coast. I love being with you, Marianne."

"And I with you, my love. You have made me so happy and in this safe space I feel as though I'm finding out who I am... Where are we going?"

"Do you see that opening?"

"Yes."

"We are going there, and then will travel up into the Sea of Cortez, find a deserted island… and then you can show me your other bikinis — although this is a firm favorite!"

"If it's deserted, I will be wearing nothing!"

James shook his head with a smile of pleasure. "Oh babe, we may never go back!"

Chapter 31

Engee stood in front of Nathan, while he considered the news. "Where?"

"It's an upscale home in Del Mar, north county, San Diego. Owned by his girlfriend."

"And they said only two people?"

"Yes. We were going to make contact in three days, but they preempted us."

"Okay, match them. They said it will only be him and this super girl of his, what's her name?"

"Marianne DuFay."

"You, and who is our smartest scientist?"

"I would say Moore has proved we don't have one. We need to hire. But I have an idea."

"Tell me."

"Let me take Jason. He can tap Iam's intellect and that should easily be a match for Moore."

"I like it. Make this work Engee."

"I will, sir."

***

The manicured two-acre property had an eight-thousand square-foot residence, a heated gunite pool and grass tennis court and sat on a plot just half a mile from one of the most private stretches of Del Mar's beach.

Engee and Jason entered, and a maid greeted them and showed them through. There was an artful interplay between vintage and modern pieces in the home with its double-height foyer, the open space making you feel very welcome. Marianne and James were sitting in the living room, laughing companionably. The walls were painted a hydrangea blue and a vintage pink glass mirror over the fireplace added more space to the already large room. An abaca rug covered most of the hardwood flooring, and a custom Victorian sofa, loveseat and ottoman were placed to enhance the room's sense of proportion and flow. French doors were open leading to a quaint, intimate patio and light permeated the entire space.

James stood. "Please take a seat. Would you like coffee or tea?"

Engee spoke for both. "Thank you for inviting us. Tea please."

"Of course," James said, nodding to the maid.

"We have already met, of course, but my name is Engee, I am the President of Brainwave, and this is Jason, he heads up our Artificial Intelligence group."

James nodded in a perfunctory way. "Nice to meet you both... James and Marianne."

Marianne looked directly at Engee. "I hope you are feeling better. You seemed a bit under the weather last time we met."

Engee ignored the inference and pretended the greeting was polite. "Much better, thank you."

As they settled, James looked at this young man who looked intimidated and worried about putting a foot wrong, and he warmed to him. He and Marianne had been told beforehand he was the inside man and so he understood his discomfort. He had opted for a conservative suit and tie. Engee had done the same, although hers had a satin finish, accentuated to add flare with gold cuff links and tie pin, and high heel black pumps.

Marianne wore a black dress with a low neckline and a high leg slit that showed fierce thigh-high cheetah print boots, and a matching cowboy hat. James had his usual cowboy boots and jeans, western long sleeve shirt and a belt with a multi tool.

After tea had been served Engee asked if Jason could bring their AI to the meeting. James looked at Marianne and she nodded agreement. "We will have ours also."

Engee looked troubled by this but had no grounds to object. Jason placed a 3D projector tablet on the table and Iam's head appeared.

Jason spoke. "Iam, this is James and Marianne, and of course, you know me and Engee."

Iam looked around at everyone. "Nice to meet you. Do you mind if I scan?"

James realized this question was addressed to him. "Yes, of course."

There was a small flash and James could see his picture appear on the base of the tablet and points on his face were measured for face recognition. "Dr James Moore, would you mind if I access all information pertaining to you."

James hesitated for a second or two.

"I realize this feels like an invasion of your privacy, so I would understand if you refused."

James studied Iam further, and said thoughtfully, "I think therefore…"

"Yes, how perceptive of you."

"Descartes is a particular favorite of mine."

"He was well before his time. It must have been a great source of frustration for him."

"Yes, I agree... please go ahead and access."

Engee looked at James. "I'm assuming you called this meeting for a reason?"

"Sukhi was a gifted scientist..."

Iam interrupted, "I would agree with that. Her graduate thesis was extremely insightful. Later white papers show she was on the right path regarding subconscious learning. The Dream Degree Program should let her take lead position."

James looked directly at Engee. "She's dead."

Iam paused for a moment. "Endeavour listed her on the manifest, did she go down with all hands?"

Engee spoke up quickly. "Yes, it was a terrible accident, but then bad things happen at sea."

Marianne put her hand on James' leg and took over. "We want to trade our help in putting you on the right path towards fixing the problem you have with the Dream Degree Program."

Engee sat up. "And what do you want in return?"

"Leave us alone, and we will leave you alone."

Iam turned to Marianne. "May I scan you miss?"

"By all means, Iam."

Engee looked at James and then Marianne. "Unacceptable, we require your equipment and you. A short duration of two years, with full cooperation, and we may consider your offer."

Marianne leaned forward; her eyes appeared to change color from brown to a steel gray. "This is non-negotiable. Accept our guidance and go away, or I will rain down hell on all of you."

Iam interceded. "Marianne DuFay, an artistic savant with exceptional physical and mental mimicking ability. She has a very high IQ, is listed as a Mensa, and has competed worldwide in martial arts competitions. She has no equal and is widely

146

accepted as a Sensei, which literally translated means one who has gone before."

Engee was furious and turned to Jason. "Whose side is it on?"

Marianne turned to Engee. "It? And you call yourself Engee, when you were born your name was..." referring to her phone, "Alice Blunt. Rather insensitive, Mx. non-gender or do you prefer Mx. NG."

Engee stared at Marianne, who leaned forward and put her hand to the cheek of Iam's hologram. "By the way Iam, you are a breath of fresh air — I think you are delightful!"

"Thank you miss, are you flirting with me?"

"Yes, I am, Iam!"

Chapter 32

Engee had asked for a moment to make a call to confer with Nathan, while James and Marianne interacted with Iam and Jason. She returned shortly thereafter. "I have spoken with Nathan, and he wants to verify the viability of your theory."

James said impatiently, "For the second time, the credit belongs to Sukhi."

Iam spoke up. "If you tell me, Mr Moore, I can cross reference it to anything known, and since I have consumed a vast amount of information on neuroscience, I believe I can validate the theory."

James didn't wait for Engee's buy into this plan. "Now, that sounds constructive, Iam, thank you." James opened his journal and began to read the excerpt pertaining to Sukhi's theory as to why Dream Degree went wrong.

Everyone listened carefully and when he had finished, Iam was the first to speak. "She could in fact be right. Blocking REM sleep will prevent the brain from organizing memories into some semblance of order, and that disorder will compound in time, putting a great strain on the mind. Excuse me while I partially test this hypothesis…"

James was quite shocked by this, and asked, "How can you evaluate it Iam?"

"I devour information from many sources, and this is what I was doing prior to this meeting. The information I recently accessed was in no particular order, and so I'm testing processor speed on fragmented data and defragmented data... Yes there is a 1.7 percent decrease in processor speed for every gigabyte of data. Projected out over days and weeks this would cause my system to reach a critical non-functioning point in 3.65 weeks."

James was impressed. "That is fascinating. I know the mind stores these memories in a chronological order in the subconscious. They are seen as an almost endless stack of lenticular screens."

Iam questioned this immediately. "How do you know this?"

"I've seen it."

Iam appeared to go offline for several seconds. "You gave a presentation to a group of psychology students at California State University that was recorded and posted on social media. This presentation detailed a Mind Link system. This system is working then?"

"It is, but it is not part of this arrangement. Brainwave cannot have this technology as they are sure to exploit it for nefarious purposes."

Iam had bitten in. "But that technology would enable easy brain access, and lead directly to the problem... Ah, this is what Sukhi believed as well, which is why she put forward the plan to bring about a meeting with you. I see. Was she honest about her subterfuge?"

"Initially no, but then she admitted it all."

Engee smiled, shaking her head. "All roads lead to Rome, Dr Moore."

James snapped back, "You will not get it."

Jason got up and shook his head as though he was trying to clear it. He walked to a painting that showed a Samurai warrior and studied the sword that hung below.

Marianne stood. "Get away from that weapon, now." She placed her hand on the grip of her tri-blade.

Jason turned and looked straight through them and out to the sun, his eyes filled with tears, and then he turned quickly, removed the sword, reversed it, and pulled it into himself with such determined force the blade exited out his back. He slumped forward and hit the floor with a thump.

James and Marianne moved directly to Engee, who raised a hand. "I dropped a small pill from my ring into his tea, as a demonstration you understand. Its chemical makeup attacks the medulla in the brain which destabilizes our survival instinct. It is quite ingenious really."

Marianne stopped. "James, they have something planned."

Engee smiled and walked closer to Marianne. "You are so very attractive you know. I am quite jealous!"

James repeated, "You cannot have the Mind Link."

Engee placed her phone on the table, and it was relaying video. Aunts Rose and May were sitting on a floating boathouse looking out at Lake Zurich with the Alps beyond. Classic and modern boats were competing in a race in a regatta and there were large crowds along the waterfront. People were laughing as the wind had died and the sailboats were at a standstill, with some contestants reaching over the side and attempting to paddle.

Engee continued, "Their bodyguards were given these pills. One chose to slip off the side and swim deep gulping in huge amounts of water, the other walked directly to the old town and jumped in front of a trolley. The waitress you can see waving at us now is serving your aunts. You will notice she is wearing the same ring as I am. There she goes to check on your aunts."

Marianne spoke quickly, "No, no, you must not."

Engee got very close to her and placed her hand on her inner thigh. "I will have you, my pretty."

James reached forward and struck her hard across the face and she fell back. "Kill them and you will get nothing — I will die before I help you."

Several men arrived and took Aunts Rose and May away by force. The video link ended. Engee put her thumb to her lip and noticed the blood, licking it. "They will be held to safeguard your cooperation. The two of you will come to a remote location to help resolve this with Iam. We will provide you with a full staff."

Marianne looked on at her coldly and began to talk slowly. "Police reports state that several girls pretended to befriend Alice Blunt and told her she had been accepted into their prestigious group. It was a football player who called the police as soon as it started and Ms Blunt was taken to the hospital for treatment. Hung juries acquitted the sorority and fraternity members involved, as the juries believed Ms Blunt had encouraged the event flaunting her fluid gender, and using it to seduce both males and females into having sex. Her brother was injured trying to protect his sister, and a head injury caused a coma, from which he never recovered. The case was never retried."

Engee stared at Marianne, her eyes misting slightly, but feigned confusion. "I have no idea what point you are trying to make."

"You were injured, but how many are needed to satiate your lust for revenge?"

"You are a strange entity."

Marianne stared at her coldly. "Not even light can escape the powerful gravitational pull of black holes that are often described curiously as bright. As they rip apart stars, gas, and dust particles heat as they are pulled into the void, releasing extraordinarily large amounts of light. Supermassive black holes are thought to lurk in the hearts of most large galaxies... That's what I see lurking in your heart."

Chapter 33

A private plane touched down late at night at the airport carrying Rose and May. The two operatives that accompanied them said nothing for the entire trip, sleeping in shifts, but this had not unsettled Rose, and May who had whiled away the time chatting, napping, reading, and knitting. They were handed over to Mateo and Catalina, a middle-aged couple who apparently ran Banner's estancia, that was called Rancho Patagonia.

It was dark all the way there and try as she might, Rose could see nothing. "I would always try to arrange a holiday, so you arrived during the day. One is always so excited about visiting new places and coming in late unable to see a thing does put rather a damper on it."

"I agree, but we will see it all in the morning, and be more ready for the experience after a good night's sleep."

Mateo spoke up. "This is not a vacation, you will shut your mouths and not speak."

Rose turned on him immediately. "How we treat this forced incarceration is our prerogative, and if we choose to view this as a chance to experience Argentina and its people, that is our choice. You will keep a civil tongue in your head when you speak to us or I will be addressing this with your superiors."

Catalina hit him hard on the leg and then turned. "I'm so sorry, it has been a very long day and we have three young children. We were not informed you were coming until very late — it has been such a rush."

"That is quite all right my dear. Your husband is obviously out of sorts."

May chimed in, "I will be insisting on an apology, however, I have never heard such rudeness. We have been abducted from our home, put on a very long flight that made multiple stops, but we are making the best of it, and not taking it out on anybody."

Catalina nudged her husband who reluctantly capitulated. "I'm sorry. It has been a long day, and the baby wakes every two hours."

Rose smiled and leaned forward. "Thank you, Mateo. Now would one of you tell me a little about where we are going."

Catalina smiled, pleased that all was now well. "We live and work on the Banner estancia, a one-hundred-acre large farm in Patagonia, which is right at the southern tip of South America. It is October, so you are here in our summer and we are in the lambing season right now."

May had stopped knitting. "Well, I never. We have come a very long way, Rose."

"Yes, but can you imagine the landscapes I will paint."

Catalina turned a little more in her seat. "The land is beautiful, flat and the pampas is very green. This is the driveway now." Dogs ran to greet them and some preening peacocks. "We have cattle, sheep and horses."

Mateo collected their bags, and they were shown in. It was like a family home, with rickety wooden furniture, chintzy upholstery and curtains on hooped runners. There was a lounge with cow leather seats encircling a wood burning fire with an old man and woman sitting companionably, both of whom smiled a happy welcome, showing they had no teeth.

Rose and May nodded and smiled back, May with a wave.

"Good evening to you, sir, madam."

Mateo spoke up. "These are my parents. They stay with us as they are too old to work."

Rose put a hand to his arm. "That's very kind of you, Mateo, and a great pleasure for your children, I'm sure."

Catalina pointed to the dining table. "Please take a seat. We have prepared a meal for you... We don't have a choice, I'm sorry."

"How wonderful!" said Rose. "We will eat what you eat and that way we can truly experience the real Argentina and its charming people."

The meal was served by a very short wide woman who popped out to describe the dishes, translated by Mateo, all made with farm fresh ingredients. The main dish was a pancheros, a steak stew made from livestock butchered on site, followed by grilled trout taken from the river, vegetables from the garden, and then fruit from the orchard. It was all washed down with a full-bodied merlot that made them both rather heady, which May explained was caused by now being in the southern hemisphere. Finally, the cook came out with a tray holding hot drinks called mate, a very strong green tea that was quite thick but delicious. This wonderful meal and the time difference, which neither of the aunts could calculate, finished them off and they retired to bed thoroughly contented, and slept soundly.

The days and weeks that followed were spent slipping into this way of life, and it felt less like being on a different continent and more like being transported to another world entirely. In the morning they were woken with tea and breakfasted on the patio, watching cattle, sheep and horses grazing casually wherever they chose. Argentinian cowboys, or gauchos, went about their business with what appeared reckless abandon, rounding up livestock, fixing fences and shearing sheep, and they would

154

often stop to pass the time with Rose and May, giving an impromptu demonstration of their riding and roping skills. The women washed, cleaned, and cooked, always smiling and laughing — a happy people thoroughly contented with life's simple pleasures.

They never went to Erik's Spanish colonial main house, and didn't want to, although they did visit the small adjoining chapel. Rose painted giant agave stems, the dry and sprawling steppe that stretched to the distant horizon, and fields of pampas, and the snow-covered Andes that were so huge they looked close enough to touch.

Mateo and Catalina organized day trips in a horse carriage to show them hanging glaciers, lakes, rivers and waterfalls. They toured the once mighty Jesuit Missions and on one trip up into the Andes to see a mountain vista, they were lucky to see a mother puma and her two cubs.

When it rained they sat in the living room playing board games with the children and grandparents, reading books and knitting. May was in the process of finishing sweaters for the children and Rose looked through the window pane, trying to capture a moment with paint as the drips made their way down in tracks. May noticed her pensive look. "A penny for them?"

"This abduction was a rather desperate act."

"I agree, it feels like a last resort."

"By someone who wants James to do something he has refused to do."

"Yes. They will soon find out how resilient and tenacious he is."

"And he is now accompanied by a secret weapon."

"Marianne?"

"Yes, indeed... Heaven help them!"

Chapter 34

The missile silo was carved out of sheer rock using dynamite in the early '60s, and manned by a crew who had been trained to ensure the enemy was destroyed as they were doing the same. Despite all the renovation, it was still a cold, dark and eerie cavern with an air of tension still present after all these years.

In a conference room in the depths of this missile silo, a different stand-off was taking place. Erik sat opposite James and Marianne, pulled a coin from his pocket and placed it with careful deliberation on the table. "It is your choice. Cooperate, or one of your aunts will die, and die badly."

James did not flinch. "Can you imagine the excruciating torment the crews in these silos had to wrap their minds around. If given the order to launch, they now knew their family was already obliterated, and life as they knew it was over. Marianne this is Helen's father."

Erik turned on his political charm. "Nice to meet you, Marianne. James neglected to mention, I am the incumbent governor of California, and have recently announced I am running for president."

Marianne nodded her head in apparent admiration, and Erik believed he had found a receptive listener. She looked at him questioningly. "If I kill him, will they care?"

Erik was taken aback, and James was undecided, as he weighed up this option. "I suspect they would. The temptation is great, but I regret we may have to forgo the pleasure."

Erik leaned forward and raised his voice. "You know me of old, and you know I do not make empty threats. We have your aunts, and I will kill one, unpleasantly, unless you do my bidding."

Marianne leaned forward. "He might be the one."

Erik decided to ignore her; she seemed unbalanced. "Complete this assignment and fix the Dream Degree technology and I will guarantee the safety of your aunts, and the two of you. We don't want the Mind Link, just our tech, working with no side effects."

"Why?"

"It is the central pillar of my presidential mandate. The education problem goes well beyond student loans. The cost of an education here in the US is a multiple more expensive than anywhere else in the world, and education leads to innovation, and that is how we maintain our innovative edge. Seriously, if we could put aside our differences and history for the moment, can you not see how much people would benefit from this. You know better than most, you were an educator."

"On this subject I agree completely. As a concept, it is brilliant, and could have a major impact on humanity. Life is a relay race in which one generation has to hand-off to the next, and each time, the information transfer gets larger. Marianne and I have evaluated this project in great detail now and have determined the rollout of this is at least five years out."

Erik's head slumped showing extreme disappointment.

"I realize this is well outside your window."

Erik shook his head. James waited, and finally added, "Unless."

Erik grasped for the possible lifeline. "Unless?"

Marianne took over. "It would require a very large

157

investment to accelerate the development. We would need to ramp up personnel, eight times what we have at present, a lot more equipment, and we would need a much larger facility."

"That would not be a problem." Erik was exuberant.

James looked doubtful. "But the investors, the board, surely you would need approval? And Nathan, wouldn't he need to buy in."

"Nathan would not be involved in this, and I carry the full voting rights of the board."

James looked doubtful again. "But how can you guarantee our safety, and my aunts?"

"I can. One word from me and it will be done."

"But how could I ever trust you?"

"If you two can expedite this to fulfill my mandate, it will secure my run for president, and then you can have whatever you want."

They both studied him, and Marianne looked to James. "Is this the high-value target?"

"I believe it is. I knew if we held out long enough."

"Would this counter their hold?

"I'm sure it will."

Marianne stood and looked very pleased. She flipped over the desk like a gymnast, grabbing Erik's head on the way down and slamming it hard into the table three times. He was out cold.

They moved with a single purpose, cleared the long trolley, placing him on it, ripped open his shirt and attached fake sensors. An intravenous pole was erected, a fluid bag attached, and the tube taped to his arm. An instrument was pulled out from underneath and James activated a preset program showing fake vitals and giving off beeps. They both put on surgical hats and masks to complete their covering and wheeled him out at a run straight to the first security station.

James shouted, "It's the governor, he's had a heart attack. We must airlift him immediately."

The guards were stunned for only a moment, but when they caught sight of Erik bleeding from the nose and mouth, not enough could be done to speed his passage onto his waiting plane.

Chapter 35

Once airborne, James and Marianne pulled off their medical gowns. Marianne went to give instructions to the pilot while James waited for his call to go through. "Hi Ferko, it's me, James, we got away."

"Thank heavens! Well done, James, are you both okay?"

"Both good, thank you. What's the update?"

"We've mobilized The Collective to look for them, but it's your friends JP and Pete who have come up with our best lead yet. Erik has a home in Argentina, Pete went there, and he believes he has seen them."

"Great news. We have Erik, and he owns and controls Brainwave. So, we should have equalized the odds. Please tell Pete to observe only, do not attempt a rescue alone. And to look after himself."

"Good, yes. I will."

"They will try to track this plane the moment they realize we've gone and abducted Erik. Can you access jet records, disable tracking, we must hide him."

"Easy, consider it done. Any ideas where you'll put him?"

"I have an idea I'm mulling over."

"With that much power and money, he will be hard to contain."

"Yes, I know."

"Drop him in a hole and throw away the key, unless you know someone who is incorruptible?"

***

Nathan and Engee came out of the lab with little to no news to report. They entered the conference room to find it empty and then noticed the blood on the table and floor. Engee called out, but there was not a security officer in sight. She and Nathan had to backtrack all the way out of the silo and into the house to find them, all talking about the emergency and pleased with their response to a crisis.

Nathan and Engee listened as the story was relayed, and they shook their heads, Engee putting her head in her hands with disbelief. The agent picked up on their distress and tried to reassure them. "The paramedic was a very capable guy and said he was sure that Mr Banner would be fine."

Engee pulled her hands from her face. "Go away."

Nathan was in a panic. "Do something Engee. Track the plane, radio the pilot. Do something."

Engee was giving instructions to her group who had now realized all was not well. "I'm working on it; the plane has dropped off radar and its ID has been disabled. That fucker."

"Who?"

"Both of them."

"Where will they go with Banner?"

"Mr Banner."

"This is not the time Nathan."

"This is not the time, sir."

Engee was talking to herself. "We don't know where they'll take him, but we know what he wants."

Nathan picked up on this train of thought. "The aunts are safe; we need to get Erik."

"No, we need to move the aunts."

Nathan was offended by the contradiction. "No, we don't need to move them."

"Yes, we do."

"Engee, you are forgetting your place."

"I will fly down immediately and move them to the superyacht."

"I'm not playing right now, Bunny."

"Neither am I. I report to Erik, as do you, and we can't get him back if we don't have the aunts."

"You think they'll want to trade?"

"No, and we don't want to trade either."

"Why not?"

"If we trade the aunts for Erik, how do we force them to work?"

"I don't understand?"

"That's because you're stupid, you have no fucking balls..., and while we're on the subject, you really do have a very small dick — and I'm not playing right now, either."

Chapter 36

About one thousand, two hundred miles west of the Alaskan Peninsula sit the Aleutian Islands — a sea-sculpted coastline with mile after mile of rugged windswept landscape endlessly battered by huge waves. It was relatively calm today, but this crescent shaped set of islands separating the Pacific Ocean from the Bering Sea was set to host yet another storm whipped up by the dynamic environment created by these two huge forces at play.

Asangis sat in his small, narrow kayak between his island and the next, as this served as a migration route for endangered whales, and he would often come here to commune with them. It was a lightweight, highly maneuverable craft. The framework was made from washed-up driftwood and whalebone and then covered with sealskin and sewn with sinew. Across the upper part of the boat was sewn a cover made from sea lion guts with a hollow hem made with leather string running through it that could be tightened or loosened like a purse around him so as not to let in water.

This peace was disturbed by what began as a small engine drone noise that increased rapidly as this narrow-beam gloss black carbon fiber, V-shaped bottom power boat came cutting through the waves driven by two four-stroke V8 six hundred horsepower engines. It was heading straight for him and Asangis shook his head in disgust. "Bloody foreigners, they're sure to be Russians."

The powerboat slowed and there were James and Marianne beaming a smile at him. James was on his phone, "Thanks Ferko, we've found him!"

Asangis smiled in return, with genuine pleasure at seeing them. "Have you heard of friendly boating practices?"

James laughed as Asangis bobbed in the wake he had created. "Why don't you answer your phone?"

"It makes noises, so I turned it off."

"It is good to see you, my friend."

"You too, my brother."

Asangis turned to Marianne. "Has this crazy man married you yet?"

"Not yet!"

"I'm available! And I have my own island!"

"I'm flattered, and very tempted, but I'm head over heels in love with this Englishman."

He smiled. "What brings you two here?"

"We wanted you to look after a package for us, to hide it?"

"I will wrap it up and put it in my urine pool that I use for softening leather, no one will think of looking for it there."

James and Marianne could not stop laughing, as they looked in the cabin at the hog-tied Erik.

***

Peyton paced the floor of the drawing room in agitation and after a gentle knock Patrick entered.

"Well?"

Patrick shook his head. "We can't find him anywhere. We believe he went to see Nathan, but his office is denying it."

"Why would they deny it, why don't they just say he didn't

164

go there?"

"The press is nagging for a statement. Is there something you can think of to keep them at bay for the time being?"

"That is not my function."

Patrick nodded in agreement, and then realized it may appear rude. "I understand, I'm sorry to ask."

Peyton walked to a window and gazed out at the rain. "When I was little, I imagined many future versions of myself. I was going to be a ballet dancer, but my teacher said I was too tall, and so my father, the governor, spoke with her and as a result I played the lead in the next three productions. Later, I changed my mind and wanted to be a journalist, and my father said no daughter of his was going to work for the enemy, and then I wanted to be a teacher and he told me, 'Those who can do, do - and those who can't, teach'. I was eighteen when he started setting me up on dates as the girlfriend of up-and-coming politicians."

Patrick was quite used to being a listener, and he leaned against the door frame, attentive as always. His husband had said a lot of people liked him as he was great company — always enjoyable to be with. Patrick learned a technique early on in life — have people talk about themselves and they will sing your praises and thank you for the great conversation. He knew she was not finished and so he nodded, thoughtfully, which was all the encouragement she needed to continue.

"Erik appeared and he got my father's full political endorsement, with his daughter thrown in for good measure. I saw politicians' wives as helmet-haired women standing silently at their husbands' sides smiling in admiration at their every word, affirming their heterosexuality, and their great devotion to their wives and children. I think I could have managed if there was maybe a good friendship, but nobody else exists other than him, and his needs and wants."

Patrick had a room full of press waiting, and this had all the trademarks of a pitiable autobiography. "You have to say something ma'am. I have prepared a guide for you."

She took it on her way out the door, knowing this little neat man was just like all the rest. Taking up her position behind the podium, she paused. "My husband is working very hard, very hard indeed, pulling together a dream team for his presidential run. He apologizes for not coming personally and asks you to please be patient."

One reporter was quick off the mark with a quip, "I hope he's not neglecting you Peyton?"

"He would never do that, quite the opposite in fact," she said with a shy smile.

The cameras flashed away, and she left, heeding Patrick's almost frantic signaling, who ushered her out of sight. "Please say no more. I wish you hadn't said dream team."

"Why?"

"Because the Brainwave miracle may not even work — and we may have to abandon it."

"But it's the cornerstone in his mandate; he's told everybody."

"I know, I wish he hadn't."

Peyton had a call and asked if Patrick would leave, and she waited until the door closed behind him. "Is that you, my love?"

"Yes, it is. I have missed you so much."

"Did you see the press conference?"

"Yes, where is he?"

"We don't know — we can't find him."

"Now listen to me my darling, I want you to divorce him

so we can marry."

"Oh, baby, are you serious? Do you mean it?"

"Of course, I do."

"Are you going to run for president?"

"I don't know, still undecided. Can you sneak away?"

"Are you local?"

"No, but I've arranged for a private jet to bring you to me."

Chapter 37

A helicopter swept in low sending the cows and horses off at a gallop. The gauchos reined in their mounts, reassuring them all was well, looking up with irritation. They landed on the lawn of the main house, and Catalina ran to greet Engee and a heavily armed guard who exited, showing them back to the house and offering refreshments on the porch. After a brief chat, she sent her staff off in all directions with instructions.

May and Rose had been taking their morning constitutional and stumbled on a set of makeshift sheep pens, with lambs birthing with such regularity, one would swear the sheep were stimulating each other's delivery. May was in the pen, sleeves rolled up, giving a helping hand while Rose held a runt who had been rejected by its mother. The maid, who had been sent to get them, curtsied, and uttered her instructions in broken English, and May washed, and they followed her to the house.

Catalina introduced Engee to Rose and May, giving her no title. "We are to leave immediately. I have given instructions for your things to be packed. We will be going directly to Santiago, where we will board a superyacht."

They said nothing in response, trying to take in the abruptness of this departure. Rose looked on at this young woman who was trying hard to hold a relaxed demeanor. "I see James is turning the tide, May dear."

Engee said nothing. May watched her as she uttered something in Spanish, impatiently. "He is a very reasonable man, our James. I suggest you stop provoking him and just ask for his help, with no demands. He will buck you if you push him."

Engee turned to face them. "What was he like as a child?"

Rose answered. "You would have to be a friend of ours for me to answer that, and you are far from that. What troubles you so?"

Engee looked at her coldly. "Nothing. You should be focused on your problems. I may have to kill you both if he and that idiot girl don't stop."

The penny dropped. "Ahh, it's Marianne."

They came out with the bags, and they all walked towards the helicopter. Engee turned and with irritation asked, "Who are you people?"

"We're people you should have left well alone. You are not very happy, are you? What made you so cold. You're like the ice queen going down to the garden's of the dead."

Engee turned quickly and pulled her knife. "I will kill you old lady, without a second thought."

Rose didn't move, and May moved to her sister's side. "I have had several brushes with death during the war. It does not scare me."

Gauchos closed in from all sides, rifles out. Engee told her guard to prepare his weapon. They stopped when Rose lifted a hand and smiled at the cowboys. "Thank you, but there is no need. This young lady is out for revenge, and a faster gun is coming."

"You will beg old woman, they all do."

Rose smiled. "You have no aura... And if it's Marianne that troubles you, you are right to be concerned. She has primitive, almost medieval ideas of retribution."

They continued walking and the helicopter started up in response to Engee twirling her arm impatiently above her head.

Rose turned. "Apparently, May, Marianne is coming to visit."

"Oh good, I've been knitting her one of those midriff sweaters she likes."

***

Erik sat with Asangis in his sod-covered subterranean home near the warm hearth where food was cooking. It had been a long, cold day, and Erik was trying to detangle a fishing net while Asangis sat in a low chair smoking a reed pipe. Erik wore clothes made from animal skins, his hair was greasy and his skin a grimy color. He threw down the net in frustration.

Asangis came out of his daydream. "If you don't work, you can't eat."

"Haven't you got another net you could use?"

"Yes, but I need all my nets working."

"For fuck's sake!"

Asangis twirled his hands in a spiritual way. "As you do this, you are detangling the mess you have made in your life."

Erik gestured in all directions. "I can see you've been really successful."

"Maybe I've enriched myself with the things that can't be seen."

"You are looking at a successful man. I work sixteen-hour days, I've accumulated a vast wealth, and moved myself into a position of power."

"You will take none of those things with you, but from what I've seen of you, you will take greed, lust, envy and pride

170

with you — in abundance."

"I see where you're going. And what have you worked on, let me guess. Patience, temperance, humility, kindness. All the weaknesses."

"My people have a saying."

"I don't want to hear it."

"The easy-hard rule. You have chosen the easy path and so you will have a hard life. If you had chosen the harder path, you would have had an easier life."

"I can see that rule is really working for you!" he said with a laugh. "Look, how much is a new net?"

"I don't like going to town."

"I will buy you twenty new nets. I will also buy you a real fishing boat — motorized with a cabin."

"Where will I get the gas?"

"We will stockpile gas here for you, for six months, and arrange a resupply." Erik watched as he contemplated this. "And I will get a contractor out here and build you a normal house, instead of this piece of shit."

"You offer to make my life in this world better, and then I will suffer in eternity."

"Why would you suffer?"

"He is my brother."

"Don't be stupid, you don't even look alike."

"He's my soul brother."

"Didn't you just meet?"

"We have always found each other in previous lives. My wife found him this time."

This encouraged Erik. "When does she return?"

"She's dead."

"You have such an addled brain, and you're not rational."

"The white woman says you have wasted your time here, and you are a forgotten soul."

Erik's head jerked up. "The white woman, good, yes, let me speak with the white woman."

"She's dead."

Erik's head dropped and he shook it from side to side. "Do you know anyone who's alive?"

"You are alive, but dead in this world."

Chapter 38

Peyton sat at her dressing table finishing the last of her make-up. This was a pivotal and yet liberating moment and she felt its weight. Erik was still missing but her lover was very serious about them being together. She would jump ship, but in a strategic way. The public would understand once she explained.

Patrick knocked on the door. "They're ready for you…" He hesitated. "… Do you need help with your speech? I could check it."

"No, I'll be fine."

She entered the press room and took out her prepared notes. "I asked my father, a former governor and thirty-year state senator, if I could continue my career once I was married to Erik and he replied no, your husband is your career. I was hoping with Erik that it would be a partnership, both as a political wife and as a friend — I got none of that. When I questioned him about my role, he stated coldly, 'You're a prop, an accessory needed for the job. Being married increases my odds of being elected, and I didn't particularly care whether it was you or somebody else.'"

The room quietened to when you could have heard a pin drop. She went on to describe a politically arranged loveless marriage in which she played her role, and he played his. "I want my life back, my own identity, and so I have filed for divorce." She left the room very quickly wiping a tear from her eye, not for Erik, but for herself. As soon as she was alone she called her lover and he answered.

"Did you see me?"

"Yes, we were all watching."

"When can I see you, my darling. I know we must go slow, being sure they are covert assignations."

"Listen Peyton, we can never see each other again. Voters insist on honesty, authenticity, and genuineness, and they will frown on a divorcee, especially when you are connected to a former opponent of mine."

"Why... opponent? So, you're going to run for president? When did you decide?"

"Right now, you were the catalyst. I had to cripple Erik, just in case he returns, and you have done that perfectly. His image is unrepairable."

She sat down and the mirror blurred her reflection.

"Listen, look on the bright side. You're well rid of him!"

***

While James took a shower, Marianne leaned in to kiss him. "I'm going for a quick run."

"Okay my love, be careful."

"I will. I won't be long."

James called out, "Marianne!"

She returned to see him looking concerned. "Are you okay? Nothing bothering you?"

She smiled and kissed him again. "I'm fine, it's just a bit of jet lag. I will run it out. Be back soon."

She turned to leave, and he called after her, "Love you gorgeous!"

She paused and looked at her hands. There was a little quiver to them, and her eyes filled with tears. She swallowed to conceal the sadness from her voice before answering, "Love you too!"

The boutique hotel was in the old town of Quito, and she walked through the lobby with its soaring ceilings and beautiful original artwork. The front desk clerk called out, "Watch out for the pickpockets, Mrs Moore."

That caused a smile, and she decided she liked the way that sounded. She waved a thank you and hit the cobbled path running faster than usual through the charming early morning streets. She passed sixteenth century colonial Spanish churches and buildings and flew past the market as it was being made ready for business; her mind was tormented.

Two days ago, she had toyed with the idea of calling her former instructor, Miss Jean, a dear friend who had risked her life to help her — she was now retired. Her thumb had hovered over the call button for quite some time and then she had pressed call. Miss Jean had answered, and Marianne had explained how she was thinking of her and wanted to tell her all the news. The call had been stilted, and Miss Jean had not questioned an underlying element that she sensed immediately.

Marianne regretted the call now, as it had somehow made things worse, and she stopped to catch her breath having not realized the distance and how much energy she had exerted. She paced in a circle with her hand pressing her side to rub out a stitch, and as she looked off in the distance, there was Miss Jean walking toward her.

She was a thin older woman of around seventy. She walked with a cane carrying herself with grace and had piercing gray-green eyes. They embraced and Marianne held her longer than usual. They carried on walking under the Queen's arch with its vivid orange and white colors. Miss Jean pointed to it. "It was originally built to protect Indigenous devotees of the old chapel from the rain."

"Why have you come? All is fine, I just called to catch up."

"You are in conflict, Marianne. Tell me."

Marianne paced, hemmed, and hawed, but got to it in the end. "It's the three rules of engagement."

"Which one has you troubled?"

"Three."

"Ah ha, you love this man?"

"I do, I think I have for quite some time."

Miss Jean smiled. "Three is now stronger. You will be better than you were."

Marianne was confused. "I don't understand. One: study your adversary to know what they will do before they do it. Two: wait for the moment when you can use that knowledge to attack. Three: do not care if you live or die... That's my problem, I do care. I never did before, but I love him so much and I want to have our life together."

Miss Jean took her hand. "If you don't care whether you live or die, you can be reckless. Now, you will fight for your life... For life and love and happiness are well worth fighting for."

Marianne took this in, took Miss Jean in her arms, and cried with relief.

"By the way Marianne, I'm coming with you."

Chapter 39

The group sat enjoying their meal at the rooftop terrace restaurant that offered an excellent view of the San Francisco Plaza. They had all taken the waiter's advice and tried the handcrafted signature cocktail, which had a kick to it.

James and Marianne had ordered the mouth-watering ceviche, a raw fish served in a fresh citrus juice with a side of Andean corn nuts and thin plantain chips. Pete sat opposite coming straight from the Patagonia estancia, where he had hidden away in the main house and seen the aunts taken away. Pete was finishing a roasted barbecue guinea pig with fried potato patties stuffed with cheese. Miss Jean was enjoying a peanut sauce, sausage and egg salad and green tea.

They waited for James to start the meeting. He took a 3D projector, placed it on the table and out popped Iam, linked by video conference to Ferko in Switzerland. "You all know each other now, except maybe our master strategist, Iam, who now resides in Zurich permanently."

Iam spoke up. "After uploading myself to the new location, I set a destructive virus to eliminate my software at Brainwave."

Ferko added, "Iam has put together a plan, executed on it using The Collective's resources to get us all we need for this operation."

James was pleased. "Thank you Iam! So, what have you come up with?"

"I continue to track the yacht and it will be within five miles of us tomorrow passing through the Galápagos Islands. We will need to coordinate the execution of this perfectly. I have arranged with our Collective news media contacts for James' prime time prerecorded interview to go live at three p.m. Pacific time tomorrow, the exact same time as our rescue. Ferko was able to embed a total of twelve Collective members in the missile silo and they have extracted all the documentation we need — it is damning. Brainwave will break, never to recover, and Nathan will run, based on all predictive analysis. This will leave Engee on the yacht alone, isolated from Nathan and Erik."

Marianne spoke up. "She will kill the aunts to eliminate them as witnesses. How many Collective members did you get on the yacht Ferko?"

"Only seven, but they are high ranking, including the captain. They lead some of the security teams and are key officers on the yacht."

Iam continued. "Evaluating all eventualities, this is my plan. The yacht guards are heavily armed, and the ship has an antique cannon, a brass black powder that fires nine pound iron balls."

Pete looked intimidated. "You expect them to use it?"

"I expect them to use everything at their disposal. The chief engineer is one of our members and he has sabotaged the bow thrusters, knowing a replacement part could be obtained at the marine supplies' depot in Guayaquil. He will use the helicopter to pick it up, and we will replace the pilot, and then transport Marianne and Miss Jean to the yacht to land on the deck at three p.m. tomorrow, exactly."

James showed anxiety at this part of the plan. "Maybe I should do this part."

Miss Jean patted him on the arm. "I will not allow anything to happen to her, and besides, she has been trained for exactly

178

this."

Marianne linked her arm in his and kissed him. "Do not worry my darling. I will be fine. Miss Jean has helped me with something, and I feel good about this."

James was still not happy. "We can call it all off, and wait to see how they respond to the news?"

Iam answered, "I predict there is a very high chance Engee will do her worst. No this is how it must go... let me tell you about your part in this."

James looked to Iam. "Okay, go ahead."

"You will sail a large high performance solo yacht. I have scanned Pete Hammond's records and he has no ability on the sea, so he will be of no use to you."

Pete looked up from eating and wondered how a statement of fact had turned into an insult.

"You will be on the boat however, helping as much as you can with the diversion."

Pete looked pleased; his sense of self-worth restored.

James realized his role. "So that's what I'm doing. I'm the diversion."

"Yes. At two p.m. you should engage. Stay out of range of sniper rifles and the cannon but look as though you intend to board them. At this same time all Collective members will disarm and capture as many non-Collective members as possible and leave the yacht using all the away boats."

They all sat quietly contemplating their assignments. Iam added, "I have a special request."

James looked up. "Anything Iam."

"Can I come with you James? I will be an asset, I assure you, I don't want to always be stuck in a basement."

James smiled. "It would be a great pleasure to have you with us. Welcome aboard!"

179

Chapter 40

It was noon, the sun was at its peak, and the three-hundred-foot superyacht Black Swan was heading north approaching the Galápagos Islands. Engee had been taking a turn around the ship, once again with her security heads, trying to anticipate what form a rescue attempt would take, and what defensive measures could be put in place. The Black Swan had four decks that got shorter the higher you went up, rising to the control bridge deck that had a suite with an adjoining office for the captain. It had a wide one hundred- and fifteen-foot beam to accommodate the owner's luxury quarters isolated on its own deck, eight VIP guest staterooms, an entertainment lounge, gym, spa and massage room, helipad, jacuzzi, and a set of three cascading swimming pools that created a waterfall effect. The rear of the ship had beach decks that could be deployed to let you gain easy access to the sea — these were up in the traveling position. It also had two away boats, also stowed, and these had releasing mechanisms and motors for launching when needed.

The captain had been accompanying her on these rounds, and was impatient for them to end. "Is it possible for you to give me our final destination?"

"No, not exactly. But I would like you to follow an erratic course to confuse any tracking, but aim for the Los Angeles area."

"I will make it so."

"Thank you. Tell me about the cannon."

"It is an antique, used as a starting gun for regattas."

"But you have round shot?"

"That was purely decorative, to add to the image of old."

"Could they be fired?"

"Well, yes, I suppose so, but do you know the sequence on how to load and fire? The recoil is dangerous, and this is gunpowder, if you reload in a hot gun without swabbing out first you could set off the new powder and the gun could explode."

"Who normally handles this?"

"Peterson, a first mate, and two other seamen."

"I will need them in the forward team. Put them on a shift rotation ready to be called at a moment's notice." She turned to one of her security heads. "Have them instruct you and your team, just in case something happens to them."

The captain had a message delivered. "The chief engineer has got the needed part and will be back around three p.m."

"Good."

"If that's all, I have to return to check all is well on the bridge."

Engee waved him away, irritably. "Yes, yes. Please keep a sharp lookout, and report anything out of the ordinary. I will be in my cabin." She turned to her team leaders. "You know what to do."

They all nodded and left.

She had been awake for over twenty-four hours and knew she needed to sleep. Looking up at the crow's nest she could see a sniper and a lookout talking as they scanned the horizon with binoculars. She passed the two operatives on the port side, and looked in to see the aunts were safely secured, and all was well. On reaching her suite she fell onto the bed and didn't need a moment before she was out like a light.

***

Rose and May sat on loungers on their private wrap-around veranda gazing out to sea on what was a glorious day — with patchy light clouds in an otherwise clear blue sky with a light refreshing breeze. They had taken their meals out here to watch the sunrise, sunset, and everything in between. Rose had sketched and May had found a collection of books by Patrick O'Brian and had quickly become quite engrossed. Their suite had two spacious bedrooms, ocean views flooding in from floor-to-ceiling windows and even a grand piano.

They had two guards, who watched them in shifts. One of the guards was uncommunicative and spent most of his time in the kitchen eating or sneaking bottles out of the well-stocked mini bar. The other guard was much more pleasant, his name was Rick, and it was his shift. "I hope I find you both well?"

Rose looked up, broken from her spell. "Yes, very well, thank you Rick."

"The islands you can see off in the distance are the Galápagos."

"Of Darwin fame."

"Exactly. The Galápagos Islands had a huge impact on his Theory of Natural Selection."

May chirped in. "Yes, Origin of the Species. Although natural selection shows a process of evolution, but not the event that initiated the beginning."

Rose stared at her sister in stunned silence. "May dear?"

"Yes Rose."

"You are a dark horse sometimes."

"Still waters run deep!"

"Obviously."

Rick smiled. "Yes, it was quite the controversy at the time. It's strange to think of James Darwin sailing these waters."

They both looked at him in surprise, and May questioned. "Surely you mean Charles?"

"No, I'm pretty sure it is James. I can almost see him in the distance, ready to enforce the survival of the fittest."

Chapter 41

It roused his spirit as the large sailboat's smooth and seamless carbon-fiber hull cut through the water. She was a beauty, with a stripped back flush deck and simple interior that did not interfere with his view from far aft to the tip of the fore. Pete lay crouched in front of the cabin door, well out of the way. Iam's 3D projector was strapped to the roof of the cabin, and with every wave that broke over the boat, Pete moaned and Iam shrieked with glee.

Pete called out, "I don't see the fascination — give me dry land any day."

James smiled. "There are no bricks and mortar here to constrain you to the earth. This vessel with its wires and rigs, bulwarks and pinrails is free to escape."

"Why am I holding this line and a knife ready to cut it?"

James put up a hand and gave him a patient smile.

These were heavy winds and tall waves, and the boat was heeling. Pete had decided it was obvious he was going to die, and James laughed when he saw his face. "Racing boats have more robust rigging and hulls, watertight bulkheads, and a solid cockpit and windows to withstand these rough conditions. There is nothing to worry about."

Pete began to feel a little better until James jumped up and ran along the deck, clipped his harness to a spot, adjusted a line and then returned. "Don't worry Pete, I can leave, it has a below deck autopilot."

"I have no idea what that means."

Iam began an explanation that Pete interrupted. "And I have no desire to learn."

Iam called out, "We are still out of radar range, but it won't be long. I would come about, and make yourself seen, James."

These solo crafts didn't need a crew member at the helm, one at navigation, one trimming the mainsail, and one looking to the foresail — this is all well and good having your friends along, but the coordination of all is a challenge. James fulfilled all these roles and could reach all the lines and winches from the helm.

Iam called out, "Fourteen hundred, Captain", and then he turned to Pete with a look of superiority. "That's two p.m. for you landlubbers!"

***

The captain of the Black Swan watched as many of Engee's security detail were led aft by gunpoint and put in the two tenders that were tethered alongside. Rick came to report. "That's all of ours and as many of theirs as we could grab sir."

"How many does she still have?"

"Only ten guards, and a few crew."

"They know how to operate the ship, and they now know how to fire that cannon, but ten armed men is limited. We have done all we can without alerting them and causing a firefight, which we were told to avoid at all costs. Climb aboard and cast off."

Rick hesitated. "If I stay and barricade myself in with Rose and May I think I can hold out until they come."

"It's too much of a risk. She will use her entire force to gain

185

them back and that could get messy. This has been thought out carefully. We must follow it to the letter."

With that, they climbed in and cast off, and ran at full speed in the opposite direction.

***

Engee was in a very deep sleep and the words kept repeating getting louder and louder. She called out for him to be quiet, but he continued. "They've gone. They just left."

It was one of her security heads.

"What do you mean?" Engee sat up. "Now listen, you aren't making any sense. Explain it clearly."

"I was off duty, but I've had reports the captain and two other security heads rounded up as many as they could, some by gunpoint and some just went voluntarily and left using the two boats."

"They're coming! How many personnel do we have left?"

"Ten counting me, and yourself makes eleven, and a few crew."

"Shit." She ran to the bridge, and searched for the two boats but they were out of sight, and that's when she saw James' boat coming on at high speed. "Give me those binoculars… It's him. Can we still operate that cannon"

"Yes."

"Destroy that boat, and do we have a sniper?"

"Just one."

"Tell him to take them out."

***

Pete was watching the Black Swan and he saw a sudden flash, like a belch of light. He lifted his head to see a ball hitting the sea and skimming three times before sinking, and then he heard the crack.

James called out, "Iam, measure the interval if you would."

"Aye-aye sir!"

Pete looked confused and so Iam explained. "The light from the flash will travel fastest, the cannon ball will arrive second, and sound will travel the slowest. Did you see and hear them in that order?"

As interesting as this was, Pete felt as though Iam was missing the point. "They're shooting at us."

"Yes, but that was just a ranging shot."

"Well, that's okay then. If I'm killed by a ranging shot, I'll be sure not to take offense."

"It's right on schedule as well!" Iam was most pleased by this.

James spoke to Iam again. "Let me know when we get to two thirty."

Iam was confused. "Why?"

"Just let me know, Iam."

A second shot, and it again fell short and was in the wrong direction. Iam called out, "Seven minutes and twelve seconds."

James smiled, pleased at their very slow reload time. The boat had a self-tacking jib and he executed on this to bring them about.

Iam was plotting course and relative distance, and he knew this would take them close to cannon and sniper range, but this was part of the plan as the diversion only worked if they believed they were the attacking force.

"How's our range Iam?"

"We are skimming the limit of their range, maintain this parallel course."

Chapter 42

Engee watched from the bridge. She had considered her skeleton team and reallocated, sending two to watch the aunts, two to the cannon, a sharpshooter into the high lookout on the mast, four to patrol, and one on the bridge to control the remaining crew members who were stopped from leaving.

"Why aren't they hitting him? What's your name?"

"Stevens, sir. They are just out of range of our sniper and cannon at this time. Shall we intercept or let them come to us?"

"Stevens, you are now head of security. What do you suggest?"

"He will have to work hard to get to us, as we have the weather gauge, and we can maintain fire on him all that time. I would suggest letting him do all the work."

"Good, good. I like it."

The sailors at the helm and radar looked nervous, unused to such an assignment. She spun around on an impulse, searching the horizon and snapped, "Keep an eye out for a kayak."

The seaman stationed at the radar questioned, "A kayak? In these seas?"

Engee repeated irritably, "Yes, a kayak."

"Who should we look for in this kayak?"

"An older Native American man, of course," she said, shaking her head in frustration, still looking through the binoculars.

Stevens tried to defuse the tension, although the order seemed just as ludicrous to him as well. "Just keep an eye out for a kayak."

***

Iam announced two thirty, and in response, James altered course to close the gap. Iam saw this, Pete too, and he moved closer to Iam. "What is happening Iam?"

"He is moving inside sniper and cannon range."

"But why?"

James interrupted. "Time to next cannon shot Iam? Give me a count down."

"Ten, nine, eight, seven…"

James looked up at the sails and then tacked at a speed that would put professionals to shame. She came about beautifully, not missing a beat, the jib and mainsail snapped into position, and the speed never faltered.

The flash, ball and thump arrived all missing the mark as they were aimed at a place where they were going to be.

Iam picked up where he had left off with Pete. "This is why he has been counting time between shots, and to answer your other question, he is trying to reinforce that we are the attacking force, to help Marianne."

Pete looked at James, who appeared to be larger in size, his attention now in a heightened state, continuously calculating and recalculating the pieces in this complex dynamic puzzle. "Can you count down from ten again Iam, if you please."

"Yes of course, We are two minutes out."

"Stand by Pete, we will need your trick soon… I will be able to pull this stunt one more time, and then they'll be on to me, and I can't afford to do it a third time."

189

Pete leaned into Iam again for translation. "The first time he changed course could have been a coincidence, but once the gunner sees it happen a second time, he will know we are predicting his shots by knowing his reload time."

"I see... Do you know what this line I'm holding is?"

"It's called a drag sail. The line is attached to a section of sail we are dragging behind us."

"Won't that slow us down?"

"It has been slowing us all this time. The gunner over the water has seen our speed and is using this to anticipate where we will be. Our speed determines how much he leads his target. Hold on. Ten, nine, eight, seven, six..."

James tacked again and couldn't help but love this boat. She came around like a thoroughbred and tore off in the new direction. "Stand ready Pete, and that line will whip away quickly when cut, so be careful."

"Okay James. You're doing a great job, by the way."

James looked down at him and smiled. "Thanks Pete, stay down now. It's going to get a little hot around here."

Pete lowered himself more. "What about you?"

"I'll be fine, it would be bad form to shoot the captain!"

Iam called out again, "Ten, nine, eight, seven..."

"Cut it Pete."

The line whipped away off the stern of the boat, and Pete could feel their boat lunge forward now it was free of the drag."

James watched the Swan and saw the tongue of fire light up and he waited with gritted teeth and was rewarded when the ball went to a spot well back in the wake of their course."

"Time?" James called out.

Iam responded. "2.58 sir, and might I add, you have done very well. I have no doubt you have their undivided attention."

James spoke under his breath. "God be with you my love."

190

Chapter 43

The pilot came in low, as he was instructed. Miss Jean activated her microphone. "Land as quickly as you can, drop me off, and then leave immediately and return to the mainland."

He seemed confused and asked, "What about you?" Looking to Marianne.

Miss Jean answered, "She will leave of her own accord. Pay no heed to her actions."

They both wore long gray tunics that covered their hips, loose pants that were strapped with socks and bare feet. They looked forward and they could see the super yacht, and a puff of smoke billowed from the cannon.

Miss Jean looked at Marianne who was already in her trance, magic soaking her spine. "Marianne, I will go down the port side and straight to the aunts, and I will hold that position preventing harm. You go straight down the starboard side. We will remain fluid but go in hard and fast."

"I understand."

"One other thing. You have been taking the pain blocker but not the empathy blocker. This could compromise our safety. Leaving a combatant alive behind you, means you are open to attack from the rear."

Marianne understood all too well what this meant and nodded. "Thank you, Miss Jean."

"My pleasure Marianne. We will lock down and only come out for you or James."

Marianne opened the helicopter door, slid out and held onto the skids, waiting as it descended to the pad. She dropped and rolled into the aft section of the Black Swan and ran to the starboard side. Miss Jean exited in a more sedate way and walked to the port side. They sensed rather than signaled they were ready and moved quickly.

Marianne ran into two guards and took them from behind. She climbed one sliding her tri-blade around to slit his throat, and as he dropped, she used his bulk to leap high gaining the potential energy to come down hard and heavy on the other operative with an in-and-out jab straight through his neck.

Miss Jean walked into two guards but they were coming towards her. They stopped and were confused, and one called out, "You aren't meant to wander."

He apparently mistook her for one of the aunts. She played along. "My hearing aid is in the cabin, what did you say?"

The guns lowered to a more relaxed position and as she got close, she threw her walking stick and it hit him straight in the teeth with a crack. He went down in pain and his accomplice made the mistake of looking to his partner for a split second, and that was all she needed to grab the stick and with a twirling back hand slam it into his face. She picked up their guns and threw them overboard, took one of their handguns to back them up to the railing, and with a twisting kick they fell backwards into the sea.

Marianne moved with speed to the cannon to find two operatives and a seaman in the process of reloading. She heard a sniper rifle take three shots from the crow's nest above and was torn as to which was the greatest threat. A sealed gunpowder box was placed well back and it contained exactly-measured amounts of powder in sacks, and there were over twenty bags inside. A lighted match on a stick was within a barrel, and this was used to press against the touch hole when they wanted to fire. The percussion from the firing had made them all deaf, and were so engrossed with the process, they were unaware there could be any threat from behind. At this stage one of them was ramming a holding wad down the barrel while another thrust a wire into the touch hole to pierce the bag that was inside the barrel, releasing the powder. The third man was cutting a thin tube containing fine grain powder getting ready to insert it into the touch hole. This would conduct the flame down the hole to the large store of powder.

She opened the gunpowder box and threw in the lighted match and ran away at high speed. The bags set alight and after a short delay it ignited, powder setting off powder in a chain reaction that created a blinding flash of light destroying the entire bow section of the ship, followed by a rising mushroom of black smoke.

Miss Jean traced the path the captain had told them to find the cabin holding the aunts. She entered and noticed a large number of small liquor bottles on the counter, emptied the brandy and whiskey on a cloth, set it alight, and stepped to the side taking two kitchen knives from the counter. She reversed the blades so they were pointing up her sleeve and waited.

There was a toilet flush, and as an operative entered the kitchen he saw the fire and yelled out, "You fucking idiot, those bottles have started a fire." He put down his assault rifle, ran to the counter and began to fill a bowl with water, and when he turned Miss Jean lifted both hands and came down into his chest, leaving the blades lodged. He dropped to his knees and fell forward.

She waited for a moment to see if the other guard had heard, there was nothing, so she stepped around the kitchen to look through the balcony door and could see the other guard in front of the aunts, holding an Uzi. She was considering her options when Marianne's explosion occurred, and he stretched out over the rail trying to see what had happened. Moving quickly, she kicked him overboard. The aunts stood, they all knew each other of old, and she asked, "Where would be best to barricade ourselves?"

Rose jumped to it. "There is a walk-in closet that is sealed. I think that would work." Off they went, and there they stayed, piling up furniture and anything else against the door.

The sniper ducked his head in response to the explosion, but then carried on firing at James' boat in the distance. Marianne scaled the metal ladder, withdrew her tri-blade and was about to kill him, when he stopped, and lowered the rifle.

She paused, arresting her death blow, and asked, "Why did you stop?" He jumped at hearing her voice, having no idea she was there, and as he turned his head, he could see the blade six inches from his neck. "What?"

Marianne asked again, "Why did you stop?"

He answered in a quiet voice, and it conveyed confusion. "At first, I thought the boat out there was a diversion. But he came on strong and took such risks. Why? Is it you?"

"Why did you stop?"

"My shots got closer and closer, as I found my correction, tearing up the deck and sending splinters flying. And then, I could see him in my sight, and he became aware of me, turned, and saluted me. That's why I stopped."

"Why?"

"It's the bravest thing I've ever seen. I knew then, I could not kill him."

Marianne took his rifle and threw it into the sea. "Give me your word of honor you will stay here until it's over. Break your word, and you will die badly."

"You have my word."

Chapter 44

The aft deck of the Black Swan had a spacious beamy layout designed to accommodate al fresco dining, cocktails at sunset, parties, sunbathing and swimming, and boarding the tenders. The away boats had gone, and the space seemed lifeless, except for two guards and Engee who knew full well what was coming. She had dressed in a pair of sheer lace trousers and a chic black blazer, with a glossy raven wig tied into a ponytail, and donned a pair of neon lavender shades and a pair of towering platform heels.

Marianne had pulled off her tunic and pants and removed a small backpack. "This will never do," she said to herself, and darted into a utility closet. She emerged wearing a shimmering cyan, teal minidress that was sequined with a mock neck and long sleeves. The curve-hugging fit and thigh-skimming hemline showed off her long, toned legs, and she hopped from one foot to the other putting on silver pointed toe heels. The Black Swan was a ghost ship, and she scanned the decks as she walked aft, buckling up her belt, until she found what she was looking for.

Engee stood waiting with two guards, and paused until Marianne came closer and stopped. "I will not be killed by you."

"Good. Give up and I will spare your life."

The was a noise to the side, and the sniper appeared. He walked slowly to Engee and took up a position behind her, drawing his handgun.

Engee smiled. "You misunderstand, probably because you're a French cretin."

"I always know I have already won when my opponent resorts to insults. This is your last chance."

"Do you know what they do to people like me in prison?"

"Probably the same thing that has made you into the cold unfeeling person you are now."

"No sympathy then from you."

"I too had a traumatic upbringing, but I decided not to take it out on others. You had a choice."

"Some of us are not that strong."

"You had a responsibility to heal, to make yourself happy."

Engee smirked and spat as she spoke, "Shoot her, kill her."

Her guards lifted their guns, and the sniper quickly raised his and executed both guards in quick order with single shots to the head. He then returned his handgun to its holster and with a nod to Marianne, walked off to the side.

Engee flinched in response, not expecting this, and after recovering she changed her tune. "I give up. As I said, I will not allow you to kill me, and I will not beg for my life." She lifted her hand slowly and moved it to the throwing knife at the back of her neck, removed the knife slowly holding it by a thumb and forefinger. Marianne pulled her tri-blade, and Engee gestured she was going to toss her blade to Marianne, resigned to her defeat.

The blade was spun high and off to the side, and Marianne watched it go, and it was then her sixth sense activated, reminding her of Miss Jean's warning about her empathy. The knife sparkled in the sun and then her training kicked in to tell her to ignore anything that was not a threat. She returned her

197

focus to Engee and immediately picked up a second knife coming straight towards her heart. There was no time to evade, she put out her free hand and closed it on the blade and it sliced into her hand deep until she could arrest its progress — the pain blocker was doing its job and she didn't even flinch, responding immediately with a fast-reflexing throw of her tri-blade.

Engee made the fatal mistake of celebrating her success too early, she saw what she thought was the knife going home, since blood went flying, and so missed the flight of the tri-blade, only noticing it when it was embedded in her chest. She looked down in shock. "You've killed me, you bitch. You killed me."

Marianne walked over to see her just before the light went from her eyes. "You died a long time ago... My knife I believe," she said putting her foot to her chest and retrieving her blade.

Chapter 45

Asangis had returned from a fishing trip, and Erik collected the food supplies and loaded them into the sled.

"How much do you want for the kayak?"

"It's not for sale. I made it myself by hand. I cannot part with it."

Erik looked out to sea. "Right, I'm leaving."

"Where are you going?"

"I'm going home."

"You have no home."

"Yes, I do — I have several."

"You have houses, but you have no home. Home is where the heart is, and you are heartless."

"Right, that's it." He walked to the sea. "I'm leaving. I'd like to say it's been a pleasure, but it hasn't. Far from it."

Asangis sat on a rock and made himself comfortable.

"You're not going to stop me?"

"No. I don't get a lot of entertainment around here. This should be good... Do you want me to try and save you, or is this a suicide attempt?"

"I was in the swim team at university."

"In a pool?"

"Yes."

"Two oceans collide here. It ain't no pool."

"Why are you doing this?"

"I'm not in control of this. I asked for guidance. I asked to understand what I had done wrong, and they sent me you."

"You know, this whole ethereal crap is driving me crazy. When you die you are dead. You are alone in this world and alone when you're dead."

"Why do you think bad people never succeed in this world?"

"I don't know, enlighten me."

"People like you only care about themselves. They will never work together, for a while but it never lasts, and then they turn on each other. Good will out. Good people will work together, support one another, and hold the line."

Erik nodded with a look of contempt. "Yeah, yeah. I'll have you know; I have been extremely successful."

"How's that working for you?"

Erik said nothing.

"The white woman said she was your daughter in this life."

Erik stared at him coldly.

"You have told me what you have gained, and so I will tell you what you have lost. You threw away a wonderful gift — she is a strong one. She is loved in this world and in the next and has saved my brother James. You will die alone, all you value will be stripped away, and you will take the vices you have worked on so diligently with you. You have squandered your time here."

Erik looked confused. "I don't understand."

Clarity suddenly crossed Asangis' face, and he nodded. "I see, I see. Life is contrast and I needed to see what you have done wrong in your life to see what I have done right in mine." Asangis raised his hands high and closed his eyes, smiling. "Thank you, my love, thank you."

Chapter 46

The dining room at the High Chaparral ranch was packed full and all attending were in the very best of spirits. It was an intimate celebratory meal; JP had insisted on cooking as it gave him another opportunity to practice providing seven courses, this time in the French style, and you could feel how much everyone took such pleasure in each other's company.

James was at one end of the table, Marianne at his side with Chanel at her feet, and Iam was at the opposite head of the table, a position he considered a singular honor. Pete and Miss Jean were on one side with an empty chair for JP to join when he was afforded the chance, and the aunts and Ferko were opposite. The meal had been a resounding success and JP entered carrying a tray of liqueurs, which he served to all and then sat.

James tapped his glass with a knife and stood. "A toast... to family who are friends, and friends who are family."

The aunts ahh'd, Marianne stood and kissed him, Pete looked as though he may cry, and Iam shouted, "Hear him! Hear him!"

"I have some announcements, and I will call on you if I may, to add detail. First, to my brother Asangis," he lifted his glass, "you are sorely missed." He took a sip and set his glass down. "On this subject maybe, I can ask Ferko for the details?"

"Of course, James. Asangis dropped Erik in the town, as we asked him to, and he returned to find there had been a recall, and he had been removed as governor. His wife had done

201

irreparable damage to his public image. Brainwave had collapsed, and several of his other companies had suffered from his fall from grace."

James followed up. "The world is far better for it. And what of the Collective, Ferko?"

"It was disbanded three days ago. They were sent a final message, 'Collective disbanded, lead good lives!'"

Rose added, "It was a wonderful idea in theory, but in practice the power could so easily corrupt."

May asked, "But what of the Savant Foundation?"

Ferko continued, "It is funded by a foundation that is so flush with funds it can run on in perpetuity."

"Good. They are doing such good work."

Rose signaled to Ferko. "Have you had a chance to tell James about the licensing deal?"

"No. James, we were contacted by a research company that wanted to have an exclusive license for your dynamic clamp technology. They are developing breakthrough drugs for the neurological diseases and believe it can give them the empirical data they need during trials. I have it with me for you to sign."

"Wow! Now that is good news."

"It's a hefty sum."

"Well, that is good to hear, as I didn't get paid for my last job, and it almost killed me!"

They all laughed, and Rose stood. "My sister and I have an announcement. We have decided to take a leaf out of your book James and get a ranch."

Marianne looked concerned. "Where? We were hoping both of you would stay here."

May reached over and took Marianne's hand. "The ranch we are getting is fully staffed, runs itself to a large extent, so we can divide our time."

James was still confused. "But where is it?"

Rose continued. "In Argentina, Patagonia. Erik has been selling off his assets, and we fell in love with the place and the people. Miss Jean and Pete are coming for an extended stay. You are all invited to come!"

Iam chirped in again. "There is nothing I would not do for those who are really my friends. I have no notion of loving people by halves, it is not my nature."

James whispered to Marianne, "What is wrong with Iam?"

"He's been wanting to understand social graces, and apparently you mentioned Jane Austen. He's presently trapped in the late 1700s!"

James chuckled. "It should make for interesting conversation."

JP stood and lifted his glass and looked to James and Marianne. "To two sweet people. They are true blue, straight as an arrow."

The group broke into applause and James and Marianne were truly touched by their love and affection.

**

James woke the following morning early and the other side of the bed was empty. He pulled on his jeans and shirt and went downstairs calling, "Marianne!"

JP called from the kitchen. "She went to feed the animals. I'll have breakfast ready in half an hour."

"Thanks JP."

James walked up the hill and there she was, wearing a flowered robe, nothing underneath, her hair tied up in a loose ponytail, and her favorite boots. It was so her. The morning light caught her just right and she turned to see him, and her smile radiated such love and beauty.

He walked up to her. "You are beautiful, my darling."

"Thank you, James."

He took her in his arms. "I've been thinking." His eyes wandered to views that were given as the robe loosened. "You are, what we in the ranch business call, a top hand."

Marianne smiled, not knowing what was coming, but knowing James all too well, she knew there was something on its way. "Well, thank you."

"I was thinking. We should make this arrangement of ours, more permanent."

Marianne looked at him and lifted one brow questioningly. "Permanent?"

"Yes, we need to go and get you a ring, my darling."

"Oh James," she said leaping on him and wrapping both arms and her legs around him. The animals got caught up in all this excitement and broke into a farmyard chorus of squeals, grunts, whinnies, and clucks — that spoke to not particularly appreciating the delay in breakfast.

"And then," he said with a knowing smile, "maybe we can work on growing a few more ranch hands!"

Marianne threw her head back and laughed. "Do you want to make some little Jamesey-Wameseys!"

They kissed, and James took her bandaged hand and pressed his lips gently against it. "I love you, Marianne."

"I love the way you love me… Je t'aime énormément, mon chérie."

The End